ISAAC AND NEWTON'S APPLES

GAVIN THOMSON

MMXVIII

1

THIS BOOK BELONGS TO

_____

For Glenda, Ross and Lisa

1   No hubbub!

2   Never to be seen again!

3   The stars at night shine brightest under the
    spell of a new moon!

4   Come with me to Quasimodo's Bridge!

5   It's Uncle Ebenezer. Mr Ebenezer Strangeman!

6   Gravity Falls!

7   Ker*fluff*le!

8   Apple pie!

9   The hall of visionaries!

10 One Newton apple!

11 Our friend's electric!

12 Would you like to try my *Tricolour!?*

1
No hubbub!

"YOU SUCK, YOU SUCK!" taunts Arthur Whitton, sitting on Isaac Newman's chest and using his knees to entrap and immobilise Isaac's arms. "Had enough, *YOU SUCK?*" he continues, chicken-pecking Isaac's torso with index-fingered jabs...one after the other, after the other. "Give up, *YOU SUCK?*"

"My name's *ISAAC,*" defends Isaac with forced pronunciation, staring up at his nemesis through rapidly clouding spectacles while trying to wriggle free, but rendered useless beneath the larger stock and weight of his tyrannical classmate. "I. S. Double-A. C... *I-THUCK!*" spells Isaac, unaware of his gentle speech impediment as his *S* becomes more of a *TH* and his accent disguises his *Double-A* as a *U!*

"Exactly!" continually mocks Arthur, now beginning to move his weight up and down as if he's riding a bucking bronco, further taunting and mimicking Isaac, *"YOU THUCK! YOU THUCK!"*

Arthur Whitton, if it isn't already clear, is the class bully. He is better described as the school bully, given his insatiable appetite for picking on junior boys, sometimes three or four years below. Arthur picks on other boys in his class but seems to have a penchant for Isaac. Perhaps it is Isaac's bookworm qualities, or his immature physique, or his propensity for success in all subjects...even sports, where his excellent hand-eye coordination marks him out as an outstanding opening batsman and a dab-hand with a racket in tennis, badminton and squash.

No one knows why Arthur is a bully. He is also bright and a keen sportsman, but he has always been of a larger physique and an early developer. These traits are not unusual and are in no way the prerequisites for a bully, but this early maturity has burdened him with an unfortunate condition. He stinks. Not just a mild body odour which when normally surrounded by a prep school of active boys is lost amidst the smell of stinky socks and sweaty sportswear, but an extreme odour of magnitude and notoriety. Some describe this belly-retching whiff as a concoction of parmesan-covered baked beans, influenza vomit and rotten fruit, verging on fully decayed! Others imagine this nose-clinching pong to resemble the sprayed scent of a defensive skunk, and a weapon of mass destruction...not that anyone has ever experienced this!

As such, no one wants to sit next to Arthur or be anywhere near his vicinity. There are no jaunts - the masters and matrons make sure that everyone is sensitive to Arthur's condition, but this isolation is as powerful as any jibe or name calling. Arthur, immune to his smell, spends every day by himself and this makes him sad and angry.

"Please, Arthur," begs Isaac, turning his head as far to the right as he can, trying to bury his nose into his shoulder. "Please, not the *Whitton Wash!*" screams Isaac, in vain as Arthur lowers his body and wraps his arms around Isaac's head, knowing this will force any opponent into submission, "I give in! Yes, you are the best. Yes, you can have my *Apple Jacks!*"

Arthur slowly retires, grabbing the bag of sweets from Isaac's hand - the bag of sweets not long bought from the school tuck shop. Isaac's weekly treat. Everyone helps Isaac to his feet, all sympathetic to his recent trauma and gives shaking-head dismissive looks to Arthur, who walks away carefree and with no remorse, noisily chewing a mouthful of apple-flavoured chews.

Isaac cannot help thinking, as he wipes his black horn-rimmed spectacles on his shirt hem before replacing and pushing firmly into the bridge of his nose with his right index finger, how easy it would be to put Arthur in his place. Arthur Whitton...*Arfa Whitt...Half-Wit* - but he knows this will only act as a red rag to a bull and attract further abuse. Isaac's retaliation is to surpass Arthur in study and sports so that Arthur will never outshine him. Ironically, if truth be told, Isaac has a propensity for laziness and is *thankful* to Arthur for becoming his motivation to work hard and apply himself in everything he does.

"I'm OK!" Isaac responds to his classmates as he stands by the window and draws in three long nose gulps of fresh air, "The sad thing is, guys, I'm getting used to the *Whitton Wash* smell!"

"Cavē!" loudly whispers Johnson, standing century at the classroom door, "Cavē! Magister! It's *Fairy!*"

Fifteen boys scramble around the classroom, crisscrossing and avoiding physical contact like a well-rehearsed drill. They grab yellow coloured class books from inside their desks; a green coloured Latin textbook adorned with an artist's impression of *Flavia et Cornelius* and a red covered paperback of forever-added-to Latin vocabulary references.

"Good afternoon, 6A," greets Mr Mount, class tutor and Latin teacher, gliding in like a silently slithering snake with briefcase in hand, and immaculately dressed in a brown tweed jacket, perfectly ironed and creased grey flannel trousers, and wearing the shiniest black Oxford shoes any boy has ever seen, reflecting the world about and representing decorum and discipline to the hilt.

"Goo_d af_ter_noo_n, Sir," replies 6A in unison and monotone, sounding distinctively lacklustre, all standing to attention while checking their neckties and shirt top buttons.

"Sit down," instructs Mr Mount, waving his hand like an umpire signalling four runs in cricket, "and turn to page forty-five."

Mr Mount has been teaching at Endeavours Prep School for forty-one years. He was headmaster for a brief period but stepped down when his beloved wife of thirty-two years, sadly died some five or six years prior. Mr Mount typifies the warmth of the school counterbalanced with positive discipline and respect, and his idiosyncracies best characterise his eccentricity.

He has a special desk, modest in dimension and raised just above the knee, tilting slightly forwards. His finely chiselled facial features resemble an Italian statue, particularly his Romanesque nose with ideally formed nostrils to harbour his reading glasses, perfectly perched for reading and an uninterrupted peripheral vision for watching every boy like a hawk. His skin colour is dark but gives no instant clue to origin - he could be Southern European, Middle Eastern or even North African. No one knows. They know his name is Vernon Mount which often raises a wry smile to any American recollecting George Washington's family home of Mount Vernon, made funnier when learning his middle name is Fairfax - Vernon Fairfax Mount. His parents must have had a keen sense of humour or were related to the Washington family in some way. Either way, nobody knows, and Mr Mount is happy to perpetuate his mystique.

Every master must have a nickname, and with a second name as unique as Fairfax, Mr Mount is unimaginatively shortened to *Fairy* - although there was a time before whiteboards and projectors when *Chalky* became a favourite due to his appetite for eating chalk and coating his lips with white dust, as he contemplated some problem or other.

The boys like Mr Mount, especially Isaac as Mr Mount runs the astronomy club, appropriately called *Stars In Your Eyes*. Endeavours is a boarding school and every Friday night, after *lights out*, and as a privilege to a select few, the astronomy club convenes in the chapel spire to open the discrete but specifically constructed hatch and view the universe and beyond. All viewed through the latest state-of-the-art reflecting telescope, the size of which exhausts the allocated budget for years to come.

"...No, Higgins," dismisses Mr Mount, shaking his head and pursing his lips, "that is the imperfect form, we need the pluperfect."

Isaac scratches the top of his head, rummaging through his golden blond hair and disturbing flakes of dandruff that illuminate in the sun's rays, as they fall on to his textbook like the first snow of winter, despite it being the last few weeks of the summer term. As he contemplates how important it is to rinse his hair properly next *bath night*, a commotion erupts behind him.

"Sir, Sir!" shouts Perkins, standing up and inadvertently throwing his seat back, making it topple and crash to the floor, "There's a wasp, Sir! The largest wasp I've ever seen!"

The boys require little excuse to distract them from the lesson in search of light relief, especially when orchestrated by another.

The whole third row stands up, again sending seats toppling and crashing to the floor, some boys seeking refuge on the tops of their desks, all screaming, "It's a monster, Sir! A wasp the size of Everest!"

Mr Mount is no fool. He knows every antic, every device and every scheme to disrupt his class. Boys are boys and have been ad infinitum!

"Hup, noooo!" responds Mr Mount, perched on the end of his seat with legs always regimentally together and feet side by side as if housed in a shoe box, "No hubbub!" he adds calmly, lifting his gaze while removing his glasses and searching for the mountain-sized wasp in question, repeating, "No hubbub!"

The wasp helicopters around each desk, touching down intermittently, immediately taking off as if scolding its feet, then appearing novice-like as it seems to crash-land on the next desk before repeating. It buzzes then flies stealth like, antennae moving side to side simultaneously then independently as if sensing or searching for its next victim.

Smith rolls his red Latin wordlist, much to the annoyance of Mr Mount, and swipes at the wasp, sometimes hitting the desk and partially knocking the wasp sideways. This action only aggravates and stimulates the wasp further, priming it like a loaded inoculation gun ready to inject a sting above all stings.

"Hup, noooo hubbub!" repeats Mr Mount, realising that his voice is now silent to the boys and all control lies with this yellow and black bodied flying insect.

"It's OK, Sir!" shouts Isaac as the wasp finds the window and pats it like a mime artist defining a box, "I can get it!"

Isaac picks up his school bag, laden with books and stationery, and without thinking, throws the bag at the window like a prisoner trying to escape. Everything turns from frantic to slow motion. Every boy watches in stunned amazement and with ever opening mouths and eyes, as the bag hits the window pane and smashes it to smithereens.

Silence.

Then, like a centre-line tennis crowd, the boys move their heads in harmony from the window to Mr Mount and back again, twice. Incidentally observing the wasp fly off into the distance.

"I'm sorry, Sir!" apologises Isaac with trepidation in his voice, "I didn't mean to break the window. Honest, Sir. It was an accident!"

Mr Mount sighs deeply and after what seems like an eternity, finally says, "Now where were we, Higgins?"

"Page forty-six, Sir," replies Higgins with an air of questioning.

Everyone continues as if nothing has happened until extraordinarily calmly, Mr Mount utters, "Newman. Take yourself to the headmaster and explain this incident."

Isaac quietly and nervously closes his books, packs them away and leaves the classroom like a defendant being escorted to the dock.

Isaac knows he will be punished, but at least it won't be with another *Whitton Wash!*

2
Never to be seen again!

Isaac makes his way through slim walkways, carved between classrooms, along the main covered path, through the quad and into the main house. He tiptoes past the staffroom, not wanting to attract any further attention for being out of class during lessons, and corners left into the entrance hall, crossing diagonally to stand in front of a huge yellow panelled door. The door carries no label or sign, but everyone knows this to be the headmaster's study. If the door is closed, like it is, it denotes Mr Hill is in residence. Isaac knocks at the door with three successive raps.

Mr Hill is headmaster and Isaac's maths teacher. Isaac enjoys lessons with Mr Hill and has many experiences of his kind and helpful side but knows that this all goes out of the window when something like this happens!

"Enter," bellows Mr Hill, looking up from behind a pile of green textbooks as Isaac opens the door timidly - just enough for him to insert his head. "What is it, Newman?"

"Mr Mount has sent me, Sir." begins Isaac, stepping into the study and closing the door. "There's been an incident."

Mr Hill listens to Isaac recount *wasp-gate,* occasionally nodding or rubbing his chin with his red pen, but always repeating, "Mmm, I see. Mmm, go on."

Isaac breathes a sigh of relief as he finishes his account, lowering his gaze to stare at the floor and placing his hands behind his back to keep him from fidgeting. He noted Mr Hill's Gothic-arched eyebrows when he mentioned the detail of a broken window and now sees how blatantly stupid it was to throw a heavy bag at a glass window, rather than simply opening it...

"Using a sledgehammer to crack a nut," summarises Mr Hill, rolling his seat backwards and standing up. The large bay window casts him in shadow as he towers above Isaac in his crisp green linen suit and smart red tie, embroidered with the school's yellow crest. "Wouldn't you say, Newman?"

"Yes, Sir. Very stupid," agrees Isaac, still staring at the floor and unsure of his fate. He sees that his shoes are scuffed and in need of a polish. Isaac hopes that Mr Hill will not notice and add this to his list of grievances. Isaac crosses his fingers.

"You are house captain and a prefect, Newman...with a position of responsibility, and a senior member of the school," starts Mr Hill, walking to the front of his desk and perching, placing both hands on the front edge, "and someone who should know better."

"Yes, Sir. Very stupid," repeats Isaac, nodding vehemently and slowly lifting his gaze, "I am very sorry, Sir. I promise it won't happen again."

"Yes, I am sure that to be the case," replies Mr Hill, now returning behind his desk and staring out of the window with hands cupped behind his back, as he rocks onto the balls of his feet and back again, "but this sort of behaviour cannot go unpunished," he continues, turning to face Isaac like a judge ready to pass sentence. "I think three *whacks*, Newman."

Isaac receives the maximum punishment. Gone are the days of litter-picking, lining up in front of the changing room wall for the entirety of the morning break or running *doubles* - one *double* requires you to change into your sports kit, search and gain confirmation, then change back into your uniform and search and gain confirmation again, often nullified by the ring of the school bell. Isaac has been whacked before by his dormitory master, but Mr Hill's *whacks* are reputedly harder!

Isaac says nothing.

"Fetch a shoe from beneath the safe, Newman," instructs Mr Hill, averting his gaze towards a large green safe with a central red dial, positioned to the right of the fireplace and holding a mountain of precariously placed yellow textbooks on its top surface.

Isaac bends down and grabs the nearest shoe. It is a slipper, a brown furry slipper with a smooth plastic sole and not very long. He turns and passes it to Mr Hill.

"Nice try, Newman," remarks Mr Hill, curling his mouth and pushing up his cheeks to resemble a sarcastic smile, "I think something bigger, please. Fetch the white gym shoe."

Isaac returns to the safe and pulls out several shoes before discovering the white gym shoe. He pulls it out. It seems to go on forever like a clown's handkerchief...in fact, it could be a clown's shoe, judging by its exaggerated length. Isaac spies *size fourteen* and hands the shoe to Mr Hill, watching it wobble and flex as Mr Hill grips the heel end firmly in his right hand.

"Bend over, Newman," orders Mr Hill, pointing to his chair, now wheeled to the front of the desk and placed in front of Isaac.

Isaac lowers his trousers and underpants, bends over and grabs both chair arms. He tries to relax. Everyone says it's best to relax.

"*Thwack*," slaps the *Green Flash* shoe on Isaac's right buttock as Mr Hill releases his right arm as if swatting a fly...or a wasp!

Isaac grimaces at its sharp sting but feels the pain subside almost instantaneously.

"*Thwack*," second slaps the yellow soled shoe on both buttocks, "*Thwack*," third and finally slaps the red marking shoe again on Isaac's right buttock.

"Pull your trousers up, Newman," commands Mr Hill, returning the gym shoe beneath the safe ready for the next poor culprit.

Isaac buttons his trousers and pulls up his zip. He is determined not to cry as the warm, dull throb insets. He rubs his buttocks as Mr Hill returns his chair behind his desk and sits once more.

"That will be all, Newman," concludes Mr Hill, grabbing his red pen and opening another green textbook. "Close the door on the way out, please."

Isaac pulls the door to and exhales, thinking to himself, "That was nowhere near as bad as I was expecting!"

He runs to the toilets to view his red *Dunlop-logoed* buttocks, before returning to his classroom and Mr Mount's Latin lesson!

Mr Mount gives Isaac a knowing glance, followed by a reassuring smile as if to acknowledge his lack of choice and to thank Isaac for taking his punishment with dignity.

"Take your seat, Newman," whispers Mr Mount, directing Isaac like an orchestral conductor, "We're on page forty-eight."

Isaac witnesses every boy give him a nod of support and solidarity as he takes his place. All except Arthur, whose face is beaming from cheek to cheek, savouring Isaac's misfortune.

The mid-afternoon summer silence is broken by the distinctive and welcomed sound of the school bell. Usually, Isaac and his class will move to *double maths* or *double science*, but not today. Wednesday finishes with *double woodwork*.

6A makes its way to the woodwork room, sited away from the main school in a converted cowshed. Isaac's retelling of his three-time meeting with the *Green Flash* soon becomes old news as they enter the woodwork room to see their model aeroplanes laid out for them by Mr Knoll, the woodwork teacher.

Mr Knoll is cool. He is also the senior sports master and an ex-County cricket player. Isaac spends many hours with Mr Knoll, often spent travelling and competing with other schools.

"Hi, boys!" welcomes Mr Knoll, rolling up his sleeves and doing a quick headcount before continuing, "Today's lesson is exciting. We have one more thing to do to complete your planes, and then we can take them to the games field and see whose plane will fly the furthest."

The boys swap excited glances, each one bragging about the details and additions they have made to give them a competitive edge - each one poopooing each other's design before they add the final colours and finishing nose weight.

Isaac's plane is painted sun yellow with green underwings and a red nose resembling a bird's beak. Although the balsa wood wings are cut from a flat section, Isaac adds another layer to the top surface, shaping it from front to back for a greater surface area to create lower pressure and *drag*, and induce *lift*. Others have concentrated on the shape and direction of the wings -

some inspired by *Spitfires*, some inspired by *Concorde* and others inspired by sheer creative imagination!

Mr Knoll moves from one boy to the next, assessing their plane, making notes and giving scores against set criteria. After the final plane which happens to be Arthur's with its futuristic profile, aerodynamic wing shape and jet-black paint finish, Mr Knoll leads them to the games field, five minutes away.

"Right, boys," shouts Mr Knoll, lining them five feet apart along the football pitch goal line. "Firstly, may I congratulate you on your effort and designs, and say how much I have enjoyed teaching you this term. I hope you have learnt more than just a few woodworking skills..." he breaks to allow the boys to shout *three cheers* before continuing, "...thank you, boys, thank you. Secondly, the proof is in the pudding! So, when I call your name, I want you to propel your plane."

"That seems unfair, Sir!" shouts Johnson, looking to his colleagues for support, "Surely we should send them all together...under the same conditions?"

"Yeah. He's right, Sir!" adds Arthur, normally the first to contradict his classmates, but not wanting to suffer any disadvantage, "We should throw them all together."

"Very well," responds Mr Knoll, beginning to see their sense. "Let's have a show of hands in favour of throwing together."

It's unanimous.

"Right you are," concludes Mr Knoll, "On the count of three. One...two...three...take-off!"

Every boy has a different recollection of events, but it is very clear in Isaac's mind! Just as Mr Knoll shouts *one*, there is a rustling in the trees behind as full leaves sway in a virgin breeze. On the count of *two*, this breeze begins to brush the back of Isaac's head, blowing his golden blond locks forwards and likening him to a Roman Emperor or a sixties Beatnik. And by the count of *three*, this miracle breeze is racing past and taking their planes on their maiden flight...high into the summer air...high into the summer sky. They have *take-off!*

"Wow," all the boys shout, chasing after their planes. "Look, Sir. It's amazing!"

All are assuming that reaching the edge of the penalty area will be an achievement, but they easily surpass this milestone. And so is the halfway line. Then some planes begin to turn and change direction, and some begin to swallow dive and crash-land with the odd unfortunate casualty. But not Isaac's. And not Arthur's. Their planes carry on without disruption and even appear to be accelerating.

Seeing this spectacle unfold, the boys reject their planes in favour of following Isaac's and Arthur's. Whose will land first? The whole class runs to the end of the games field, only to see both planes fly over the boundary trees and on and on into the distance, never to be seen again.

The planes may disappear from view, but not from their minds...or their conversations for the rest of term.

Isaac and Arthur are declared joint winners. Both are content not to lose to each other!

3

The stars at night shine brightest under the spell of a new moon!

Isaac returns to the changing room, still boxed and padded, and carrying his *Duncan Fearnley* cricket bat in his gloved hands. Endeavours has an important match coming up - the last match of the term and the school's first eleven has been doing net practice.

The rest of the school has been rehearsing Sports Day or at least the logistics. Masters shout through megaphones, sometimes forgetting when they turn to talk to each other, appearing and sounding like sparring ducks before they realise, lower them only to become silent film stars in the eyes of the pupils patiently sitting cross-legged in lines before them.

Back in school uniform, Isaac and his fellow cricketers stand in line for school afternoon tea. The queue seems a mile long with every Tom, Dick and Harry licking their lips in anticipation of the delicacies in store.

If ever there was an advert for not partaking in afternoon sweet pastries, it would be Meg. Meg is the kitchen hand. Dressed in a grey pinafore with matching grey apron to match her grey sweptback bobby-pinned and *bunned* hair, and her grey wrinkled face, she supports a gummy smile without a tooth in sight!

Meg suffers no fools, and although she terrifies the boys, her strictness brings efficiency, and it's not long before Isaac is sat munching a freshly baked apple doughnut and sipping a fluted plastic beaker of cool freshly made lemonade. Four o'clock heaven.

After a round of croquet, the five o'clock bell rings for *chapel*. Like rabbits scurrying back into their burrows at the sight of an overhead hawk, boys are drawn like iron filings to the magnet of the school chapel. This modern interpretation of a church is large enough to hold the entire school and instil a sense of security and unity.

Mr Pike, the music teacher, bashes out the tune on the grand piano as the choir leads the congregation through the Endeavours school anthem. A small sermon from Mr Hill is accompanied by a *reading*, always delivered by one or more of the senior boys. Today it is Isaac's classmates, Johnson and Higgins.

The school watches and doesn't always listen, but today they do!

Johnson and Higgins stand side by side and introduce the reading by chapter and verse. Higgins begins and belts out his words with confidence and clear diction, only for Johnson to begin nudging him - once then twice. Higgins realises his oversight, stops and sits down. He has read some of Johnson's verse!

Johnson, rather than carry on from where Higgins left off, begins his section again, only to find this mildly amusing. This mild amusement grows from a smile into a snigger until Johnson completely loses it and breaks out into uncontrolled laughter. The whole school laughs too, like a symphonic movement of happiness and release. Even some of the masters join in. But not Mr Hill or Mr Pike. Laughing in *chapel* is sacrilege.

As the boys exit the chapel like a rewound water fountain, Isaac sees Johnson being reprimanded. He learns later that Johnson is banned from ever *chapel reading* again. How unfunny is that!

First prep begins at five thirty, as boys assemble in their classrooms to begin forty-five minutes of homework. Forty-five minutes isn't long, but when the sun is still shining and teasing, it drags on. The bell rings, and the whole school descends on the dining room. Supper. *Second prep* begins at seven and lasts another forty-five minutes. Then a series of staggered bells denote different bedtimes. Isaac's is last, sounding at eight thirty, giving thirty minutes to prepare for bed and *lights out* at nine.

The dorm is hot and sweaty, and Arthur's stench seems even worse, as boys in single beds and double bunks try to fall into the land of Nod - some reading by torchlight, some secretly listening to music, most whispering to their neighbour before the energy of the day's activities is finally spent, and dreams replace reality.

It's probably not much later than half-past ten, but the boys are in a deep sleep. Mr Hummock, the dorm master, gently opens the door and approaches Isaac. He nudges Isaac by his shoulder until Isaac stirs and without any introduction, simply whispers, *"The stars at night shine brightest under the spell of a new moon!"*

Isaac rubs his eyes and still slightly dazed, responds, "What's that, Sir?"

"The stars at night shine brightest under the spell of a new moon!" repeats Mr Hummock, exiting the room as he sees the penny drop on Isaac's face.

It's *E-Day!*

This code is given to all E-Day team leaders, of which Isaac is one of three. Endeavours has three *houses* - Galileo, Newton and Einstein, named after pioneering astronomers to fortify the school's motto of *Extende Ad Astra*, translated as *Reach For The Stars.* Galileo sports the colour yellow, Newton, the colour green and Einstein, the colour red. Isaac is Newton.

E-Day, short for Endeavours Day, is only for the senior boys with middle and junior boys enjoying their manifestations earlier in the term. The boys have been preparing all term, once a week traipsing into the school woods to construct a habitable camp from locally sourced materials and clearly define a boundary to encompass an area for cooking, a ready-to-light campfire and adequate fortifications to protect themselves against other teams. They also prepare a handmade raft for the *What Floats Your Boat* competition held on *Inner Wood Lake.*

Isaac awakens his team as quietly as possible. They change into jeans, team-coloured shirts, trainers, a waterproof jacket, collect a boxful of provisions and campsite paraphernalia from the school kitchen, and line up on the playground by eleven p.m.

There is no new moon, only a full moon, highlighting excited faces, some of whom have *double-fingered* each cheek with black boot polish and tied team-coloured bandanas around their heads to resemble *special forces* commandos rather than young boys on a self-reliance experience!

You can bottle the anticipation.

Mr Hill blows the whistle to send forty-five yellow, green and redshirted boys to their respective camps and begin lighting their fire. This fire cannot go out and must be staffed throughout. Each camp hoists its team flag on its makeshift flagpole.

Meanwhile, Isaac divides his team, starting with Johnson. "Billy, you're in charge of the fire and protecting the flagpole. You six will protect the camp. You four, headed by Arthur will raid Galileo and us four will raid Einstein, right?" he suggests, pointing at each team member as the fire takes hold, flickering and spitting light on everyone.

Arthur pipes up. "I think I should oversee the fire, and protect the flagpole!" he says, unused to contributing, "No one will want to risk the *Whitton Wash* for the sake of capturing a flag!"

"He's right, Isaac," agrees Billy, shocked by his support for Arthur, "Arthur is our secret weapon...and why don't we attack one camp at a time? Strength in numbers and all that!"

"Sounds like a great plan!" replies Isaac, nodding his head and noting his team's full support, "Arthur, you're in charge of the fire and the flag. Guard it with all your stink!" He pauses to smile and pat Arthur on the shoulder as everyone laughs and gives Arthur a friendly nod, which immediately makes Arthur very happy, before Isaac finishes, "You six take your positions around the camp and you seven get ready to come with me."

The klaxon sounds the beginning to *Keep The Flag Flying.*

The camps are spaced a fair distance apart and create an equilateral triangle in plan view. The teams have no maps and must navigate their way through familiarity and under the disguise of darkness. If another team tags *you* then you must return to your camp and begin again.

Isaac takes his raid party to the right, darting from one tree to the next, sometimes crawling on all fours and using fallen boughs to hide behind. It's not long before they see the flicker of the next camp. Camp Galileo.

"I reckon they'll only be expecting four of us," begins Isaac, whispering, "so let's split into two groups of four. You four, create a decoy to the left and us four will surprise them from the right."

Billy takes one raid party around to the left, trying not to be seen or heard, to hear shouts from camp Galileo, "They're over there," and "I can see Newton."

To help matters, Billy can see a raiding party from Einstein also creeping up on his side, again hearing shouts from camp Galileo, "This side, guys," and, "That's definitely Einstein."

Meanwhile Isaac and his raid party edge closer to the right-hand side, ready and waiting for the right time.

As Billy and Einstein rush the camp to meet a wall of Galileo, three of Isaac's raid party run towards the Galileo flagpole and akin to *the evolution of man*, create an ever-increasing ramp of bodies. Isaac runs in and steps from one back to the other, leaping into the air to grab the Galileo yellow flag, then landing with a forward roll and heading back out of camp with the others before Galileo can begin to compute what's happened!

Isaac ties the yellow flag around his waist and waits for Billy and his raid party to join them. Billy arrives single-handed. Three of his team must return to camp Newton and begin again.

"Let's not waste time waiting for them," suggests Isaac, "let's strike while the iron is hot...while everyone is regrouping."

"Excellent idea," replies Billy, all five boys placing a single hand on top of each other's as they huddle, before Isaac whispers loudly, "Go, *Newton Force*. Go!"

"Go, *Newton Force*. Go!" they repeat, raising their collective hands into the midnight air.

As before, Billy and another boy move to the left of camp Einstein and act as a decoy while Isaac's raid party rushes in from the right. As planned, they have caught Einstein napping, and their red flag is yet to be captured. Instead of creating a ramp, Isaac's raid party turn five feet from the flagpole, stand side by side, place one knee on the ground and interlock their hands to create a footstep. Isaac runs in, places his right foot on to their *step* as they launch him into the air to grab the red Einstein flag!

Isaac walks his victorious raid party back to camp Newton to join the others also in celebration. Arthur was right - no one wanted to risk a Whitton Wash so early into E-Day!"

Isaac takes the yellow and red flags from around his waist, lowers the Newton green flag and hoists all three to rapturous applause!

"Go, *Newton Force*. Go!" they all shout, as they stand around the campfire and warm their hands as if cooking marshmallows, "Go, *Newton Force*. Go!"

4

Come with me to Quasimodo's Bridge!

"How did you sleep, Billy?" enquires Isaac, prodding the fire with a knobbly branch before throwing it on to the quietly smouldering campfire and bringing it back to life. It is his turn to watch the fire.

"As well as can be expected…" smiles Billy, exiting the camp and lowering the hatch door once more, "…sleeping on a floor of dried bracken with a rolled up waterproof jacket for a pillow!" he adds, stretching and yawning the loudest yawn Isaac has ever heard. "It's six o'clock. My turn to watch the fire. Why don't you get some kip, Isaac?"

"It's not worth it now," replies Isaac, giving up the fire *seat* to Billy. "The breakfast klaxon will sound in half an hour, and then it's all-hands-on-deck!"

Isaac and Billy sit chatting, reminiscing over last night's victory and swapping stories of the night-visiting spiders and creepy crawlies.

The Newton camp resembles a sperm whale with a large, curved backbone rooted at one end, two curved yokes resembling a jawbone at the *mouth end*, and a dozen or so supporting ribs down both sides. Although they aren't allowed to use any materials from outside, Mr Knoll supplies each camp with a stack of used plastic fertiliser bags, a hammer and a bucket of nails to create a waterproof inner membrane before covering it with interlocking branches and stuffing with bracken - refreshed each week to make it seem alive and kicking, and camouflaged in its natural environment. They nickname the camp *Moby Dick*, and with fourteen boys sleeping *head to toe* inside, it seems more than appropriate!

The klaxon sounds like a cockerel crowing the break of dawn - a cockerel with a dickie stomach!

Isaac opens *Moby's* hatch to wake up team Newton. Like opening a jumbo jet's door at the end of a long-haul flight, the outpouring odour slaps Isaac in the face as if challenging him to a duel. Fourteen *Arthurs* stir and leave Moby Dick - whose job of providing overnight accommodation is now complete.

A few of the boys grab the metal shovel from the paraphernalia box and disappear into the distance to do what comes naturally!

Mr Mount suddenly appears like *Mr Benn's* shopkeeper. Isaac is shocked to see him in casual clothes, although his jeans still possess the crispest crease and his yellow, green and red checked shirt shows the folds of a brand-new purchase. Isaac's heart skips a beat when he spies Mr Mount's *Green Flash* shoes, again brand-new and a familiar huge size - size fourteen if Isaac isn't mistaken!

"Morning, camp Newton," begins Mr Mount, holding his clipboard to his chest and peering over his reading glasses, "I trust you all slept well?"

"Like a log!" replies one boy. "Never better!" replies another. Both are lying through their teeth!

"Very good. Very good!" responds Mr Mount, unaware of their sarcasm. "Anyone feeling ill or in need of medical attention?"

"No, Sir," replies Isaac, shaking his head and looking at the other boys for reassurance, "We're all good. Thank you, Sir."

"Very good. Very good. Then I suggest you crack on with breakfast. *Seek, And You Shall Find* starts at eight. My tip is not to get greedy and dip into your lunch rations...you'll be staving by then...and tired. I've seen many a camp fall into an argument over food!" he concludes, heading off in the direction of camp Einstein.

"Who wants to cook?" Isaac asks, grabbing the box of provisions and taking out the plastic-wrapped parcel, labelled *Breakfast*, "And who wants to make tea?"

Arthur volunteers to be *camp chef* and Billy pronounces himself, *Mr T!*

"I don't know what Mr Mount's going on about!" declares Isaac, wiping the last smidgeon of baked beans from his bowl before licking it like a dog, "I'm stuffed! Bacon, eggs, baked beans, four rounds of bread and two beautifully cooked sausages! Well done, Arthur," congratulates Isaac, grabbing his mug of tea and downing the remaining six gulps, "And that's the best brew ever, Billy!"

Everyone agrees and begins to clean up. Some take responsibility for the cookware, some for the bowls, plates and cutlery, some for cleaning inside the camp and some for tidying the campsite. Mr Knoll will visit shortly to inspect and mark. It all counts to the final score - a score, Isaac and Newton are determined to top.

Mr Knoll comes and goes in silence - his face, deadpan and scores, close to his chest.

The eight o'clock klaxon sounds. Isaac sends George Wilton to collect the first clue from E-Day base camp, situated in *Mower's*

Meadow next to *Inner Wood Lake* and where the masters have pitched their shop-bought tents and gas-fuelled BBQ!

It's called *Mower's Meadow* because the grass is so perfect and it resembles a beautifully mowed lawn.

George returns, waving the green envelope in the air before handing it to Isaac. Everyone is sitting around the campfire and waiting to put their grey matter to work. Isaac reads the first clue aloud.

To the stars we reach
Sometimes poles apart
Is it science or is it art?
Only one is perfect beech!

Silence. Billy offers an idea only to encounter shaking heads. Some boys become distracted, feeling uncomfortably clueless. Isaac has a flash of inspiration. "*To the stars we reach* could refer to the telescope in the chapel spire," he begins, everyone nodding and liking his train of thought, "and *Sometimes poles apart*...I know when Mr Mount calibrates the telescope he must find two points of reference, aligned to each other. He mentioned an old pine tree, stripped of all its leaves and branches, standing high in the woods near Oxbow field. If you draw a straight line between that tree and the chapel, it runs down the side of Oxbow field..."

"I've seen a solitary pole there," adds Billy, "I thought it was a disused telegraph pole, relieved of its fixings..."

"That's right," confirms Isaac, continuing, "*Is it science or is it art?* Must refer to that *perfect* machined pole as *science* while the pine tree is *art*...and if I'm not mistaken, the Oxbow pole is made of *beech!*"

"The next clue must be attached to that pole," suggests Arthur, getting to his feet, "I'll run and fetch it."

The Oxbow pole is some distance from the camp, but as a team, they have decided to remain in camp rather than everyone venturing from clue to clue - allowing them to stay calm, reserve their energy and have access to refreshments.

Twelve minutes pass before Arthur returns, grasping another green envelope. They know that there are six clues in total and they have two hours to complete the task. Staying in camp might backfire - only time will tell.

"Well done, Isaac," shouts Arthur, puffing and panting, and grabbing his knees to steady himself, "Inspired deductions!"

It's the first time Isaac has ever heard Arthur say something positive to him!

Isaac reads the second clue. After further deliberation, Billy works out that there is a cow feed trough over in *Narrow field*. One of the other boys runs the round trip to return with yet another green envelope. This procedure continues clue by clue until Isaac has the last clue in his hand with only sixteen minutes remaining. It's going to be tight!

From tooth to tooth
And nose to nose
Strings are stretched
The toll of friendships formed

Isaac doesn't know where it comes from, but after five clues, his brain is tuned and targeted. "It's a bridge!" he declares, "...between two teeth...the bridge of your nose...*strings are stretched* on a violin bridge, and *stretched friendships* are bridged between people to make things better!" he finishes, glancing at Arthur and smiling.

"But what bridge?" poses George, "There are three bridges...*Amity bridge* over Miller's stream, *Rocks bridge* joining the two climbing rocks and *Quasimodo's bridge*, the humpback bridge on the road by the farm."

"We have to try all three, we haven't got time to take a risk on one," decides Isaac, reading his watch with ten minutes to go, "The five who have already gone, stay here. You two go with Billy to Amity bridge. You three go to Rocks bridge, and you three come with me to Quasimodo's bridge. We'll meet at Mower's Meadow. Run like the wind. We've only got nine minutes!"

Billy's group stand by the base camp operations tent, unsuccessful at Amity bridge. The second group returns from Rocks bridge, slowing as it approaches and shaking heads. Billy checks his watch. There are ninety seconds. Galileo and Einstein are nowhere to be seen which is reassuring, but no Isaac neither!

Sixty seconds.

Then through the gate sprints Isaac, holding a green key. He arrives without saying a word, enters the operations tent and inserts the key into the single black box on the table. The key turns just as the klaxon sounds and inside the box are fifteen glossy toffee apples. Morning tea treat!

At ten forty-five the klaxon sounds again. All teams must report to Inner Wood Lake for *What Floats Your Boat*.

Each team has forty-five minutes to make any adjustments and add finishing touches to their raft.

Galileo has crafted an interpretation of a tri-catamaran with cantilevered floats on either side of a long narrow centre, on which their six-boy crew will straddle. Einstein has a traditional square-shaped raft with floats down two edges, and punting poles rather than oars for their six-boy crew. Newton has a long narrow raft with two strips of floats tied together, six old plastic seats bolted to the top, and dragon boat type oars made from filled-in seen-better-days tennis rackets.

The floats are large plastic kitchen barrels, once used for containing cooking oil, sauces and cleaning products. They come in three colours - yellow, green and red, and are divvied out to their corresponding team.

The three rafts are in line, floating at the start line by the jetty - six-boy crews primed to jump on and ready to row for their lives. The first team around the blue buoy and back to the jetty is the winner!

Isaac puts Billy at the bow and Arthur at the stern to *steer*. He will sit this one out and support from the sideline. The klaxon blows, and mayhem ensues. Eighteen boys scramble onto their respective rafts, trying not to fall in or capsize their raft. Then they're off. The remaining boys shout encouragement from either side of the lake.

Galileo outclasses everyone, as three paddles the left-side and three paddles the right-side, gliding through the water and distancing from Newton - bobbing like an apple in a barrel and struggling to steer in the right direction. Einstein goes more in circles than forwards until its crew leader takes charge.

Galileo rounds the buoy and heads for home. Einstein overtakes Newton as they vie for position around the buoy. Then Newton seems to stop, even with Billy screaming for double stroke. Newton sinks - someone had forgotten to plug the containers! Isaac can't help but laugh as his team swims ashore to Billy's cry of, "Abandon ship!", dripping like drowned rats as they all turn to watch the Newton raft disappear under a tirade of bubbles!

All teams are ordered to return to their camps, extinguish their fires and bring all equipment, including lunch rations, to Mower's Meadow. The masters will prepare a communal lunch.

After inter-team *Tug-Of-War*, entries for *Worst Joke* and *Longest Recital Of Pi*, everyone joins into a sing-song while the final scores are tallied and checked.

Mr Pike arrives and improves *Ging Gang Goolie* with stepped and repeated lines from each team, getting louder and quieter to the raising and lowering of his conducting arm. It sounds fantastic!

Mr Hill grabs the megaphone and requests quiet and attention before announcing, "And...in reverse order...the team with seventy-two points is...Einstein," he pauses as everyone jeers and cheers, "...and the team with seventy-six points is..." he pauses again, knowing that he will be announcing the winner simultaneously, "...Galileo. Congratulations, Newton! You have set a new E-Day record with eighty-seven points!"

Isaac and team Newton raise their arms in celebration and shout, "Go, *Newton Force*, Go!"

E-day ends with forty-five boys skinny-dipping in the outdoor school pool.

5

It's Uncle Ebenezer. Mr Ebenezer Strangeman!

Isaac stares out of the newly glazed class window, watching Mr Knoll directing cars down the school drive, and an ever-growing number of parents begin to parade around the front lawn and beyond.

It's the last day of term and school Sports and Speech Day.

"...Isaac," Mr Mount calls out his name, regaining his attention, "you have doubled your shares this term with one hundred and ninety-nine pence!"

Isaac *invested* his fictional one hundred pence in *Appel* shares in anticipation of a new product launch and confident they would be *a sure thing* to win the coveted book token award.

"But the winner of *What's My Share* with three hundred and one pence - an unprecedented and remarkable hike in such a short space of time, is...Arthur!" declares Mr Mount, summoning Arthur to the front of the class to receive his prize, adding with a grin, "If only I had invested my life's savings with you!"

Arthur *invested* his one hundred pence in a Scottish energy firm, on the sound of its name - *McArthur Petroleum*. He lucked out when they discovered oil beneath Loch Ness...the headlines reading, *"Monster find in Loch Ness!"*

6A spends the remainder of the lesson with a fun spelling game, Billy topping everyone with his perfect spelling of *antidisestablishmentarianism!*

Everyone is excited, and you can feel it in the air.

Isaac can't wait to see his parents. He hasn't seen them all term, and they are travelling all the way from Hong Kong to watch him compete in Sports Day and then take him on a three-week holiday to the Greek Islands. Isaac's mother and father are financiers with their own company they located in South East Asia six years ago, the full time that Isaac has been attending Endeavours. Isaac rarely sees them, envying other boys with closer parents, sometimes wishing he could swap his inflated personal allowance for more one-on-one time.

It is what it is, and Isaac has no say or influence.

There are other boys with similar scenarios, boys with divorced or single parents, or worst still, boys with one or more deceased. Isaac knows he isn't unique, but like any child his age, he hankers for reciprocated family love and security. At least today, he will feel as normal as most, and he can't wait!

The ten o'clock bell rings. A duplicated cheer sounds out in every classroom. No more lessons! Hurray!

All the boys run and change into Sports Day white t-shirt, socks and shorts, donning freshly whitewashed plimsolls, before heading out to the front lawn for pre-Sports Day morning tea. There are apple turnovers for the boys, and de-crusted sandwiches and Danish pastries for the masters and parents.

Isaac can't find his parents. Disappointed, he thinks their plane must be delayed, and it's just a matter of time before they arrive and call out his name.

Sports Day begins at eleven o'clock and is hard fought. The games field is dotted with white as events are run simultaneously, every boy competing in at least one event if not two or three. Isaac comes third in the *senior long jump* and wins the *eight hundred metres*. Newton is now drawing with Einstein, both behind Galileo with only the junior, middle and senior relay races remaining.

Einstein wins the junior relay race, making them joint first with Galileo. Then Newton wins the middle relay race to draw all teams level. It's all down to the last event - the senior relay race!

Artur, Billy, George and Isaac are *holding baton* for Newton. It's one lap and three baton exchanges. What can go wrong!?

Isaac looks again for his parents but to no avail. They will miss their last chance to see him compete. He shakes his head but dismisses his annoyance to concentrate on the task at hand. He is the fourth anchor...ready to bring Newton home!

Twelve boys position themselves around the track, while the rest of the school gathers on the inside, and the parents form a human chain around the outside, ready to pledge allegiance to one house or other. There's something gladiatorial about the whole scene - thank goodness the batons are only smooth aluminium tubes!

Mr Hill lifts the megaphone to his lips. "Who'd have thought that after nearly two hours of competition, we are tied neck and neck and only one minute from deciding the final order," he says, trying to build tension and milk this rare occurrence, the whole crowd shouting for their team before settling down once more, "Teams. Take your positions. On your marks. Get set. Go!"

Newton is in the inside lane, Einstein is in the middle lane, and Galileo is on the outside lane, with a spaced-apart start to compensate for the track's curvature. The first runners roll around the bend, with Galileo looking deceptively *miles in front* and Newton appearing to flail behind. The crowd goes wild, ironically drowning out each other!

Arthur is the first baton carrier, running as fast as he can and not wanting to let down his team. He approaches George and screams above the crowd, "Go, George. Go!"

George begins his run, holding out his left hand behind him at forty-five degrees with fingers firmly together and thumb opened out to provide a clear arched target for Arthur. Arthur stabs the baton into George's hand with his right hand. George feels it hit the top of the arch and wraps his fingers and thumb around it securely. He screams back to Arthur, "I've got it!"

Arthur releases and immediately slows down, again screaming, "Go, George. Go!"

George sprints down the back straight, appearing to gain no ground and still look in third place. As he nears the top bend, George, like Arthur before, screams to Billy, "Go, Billy. Go!" and just as before, Billy begins running with his left hand outstretched behind him. George attempts to stab the baton into Billy's hand but misses the *sweet spot*. Billy falters and begins to glance behind, grabbing at the baton - conscious of the fast-approaching disqualification mark. Billy fumbles again, but just as the worst possible scenario seems inevitable, he takes hold of the baton successfully, moving it from his left hand to his right. Unfortunately, he has lost precious seconds.

"Go, Billy. Go!" shouts George, the crowd whipping itself into a frenzy as Galileo seems to be pulling away...but not if Billy has anything to do with it. He runs the top bend like an astronaut riding a g-force simulator, angling his body to the centre of the bend, his cheeks appearing to invert under the speed.

It's very close. Billy nears the end of the bend and screams to Isaac, "Go, Isaac. Go!" thrusting the baton into Isaac's left outstretched hand. This time without an episode. Thank goodness!

Isaac transfers the baton to his right hand and focuses on the white tape, dangling chest-height across the finishing line. All three runners are level pegging, matching each other for speed and rhythm - Newman for Newton, Hare for Galileo and Rayling for Einstein. There are fifty metres to go. The crowd is jumping up and down, some hiding their eyes...afraid to watch the result.

Then thirty metres and they're still neck and neck. There will be no photo finish - it's just a school Sports Day! Then twenty metres and still no change. Then ten metres, but Rayling appears to overstride and trip, placing Einstein behind the other two.

Isaac thrusts his chest forwards, outstretching his chin like a tortoise sticking his head out from beneath its shell, and beats Hare by a cat's whisker!

Isaac wins for Newton and is declared a hero by every house member. Mr Hill confirms the result through his megaphone before concluding Sports Day and inviting everyone to lunch.

Some boys picnic with their parents around the school grounds while others join the buffet line, helping themselves to a paper plate of finger food and a fluted plastic beaker of freshly made lemonade before sitting on the front lawn.

Isaac is concerned. His parents have still not arrived, and he's starting to worry. He finds Mr Mount and relays his situation.

Mr Mount heads back to the school office to see if there are any messages or whether they can contact Isaac's parents. He reappears, handing Isaac an A4 printout. It's an email from his parents, matter-of-factly and very simply saying,

"To whom it may concern,
Please pass on our deepest apologies to our son, Isaac Newman, but something unforeseen has come up at work, and we will be unable to attend his Sports Day or indeed, take him on a summer holiday. We have arranged for Mr Newman's cousin to pick up Isaac and take responsibility for him over the school holiday. Please tell Isaac we are very sorry and that we have topped up his bank account to make up for it.
Yours faithfully, Mr and Mrs Newman."

Isaac is flabbergasted but not surprised. It happened once before one Christmas, but never for the whole summer. That time he stayed with Billy because neither his mother nor his father has siblings, and both sets of grandparents died before or just after Isaac was born. He hasn't met his father's cousin but has heard his father describe him as *one in a million*. Isaac puts on a brave face for Mr Mount.

"Are you OK, Newman?" enquires Mr Mount, always concerned when parents let down their children, "Can I be of any assistance?"

"That's very kind, Sir" replies Isaac, forcing a smile and lying through gritted teeth, "I'm fine!"

At two-thirty, all the boys are sent to change back into school uniform and reconvene on the front lawn for school speeches at three o'clock. The boys sit cross-legged towards the front, closest to the masters and the table of trophies while the parents occupy the rear, sat on chairs borrowed from the chapel.

Isaac collects the E-Day and Sports Day team trophies, watching boys about to leave Endeavours for public school pick up most of the remaining awards.

The highlight is when everyone, including the parents, falls into tumultuous laughter when a boy who left the term before on an art scholarship, donated a cup to encourage budding artists, only to receive it back as this year's *Artist of the Year!*

Mr Hill thanks all his masters for their continued support and hard work, all the kitchen and grounds staff for feeding and maintaining the school, and all the matrons and medical team for keeping the school well-groomed, clean and healthy, often providing a shoulder to cry on or at least, a very sympathetic ear! He thanks the boys and wishes all *leavers* the best of luck in their new schools before wishing everyone a fantastic summer break. He then signals to Mr Pike sitting at the grand piano, wheeled out from the chapel to lead the school through the school anthem.

Mr Knoll stands up and rallies three cheers for Mr Hill. Everyone is then free to go. It's four o'clock precisely!

Trunks are fetched in record time and with enthusiasm unmatched at the beginning of term! It's not long before everyone has left as if escaping the plague! All except Isaac, sitting patiently on his gigantic green trunk outside the school changing rooms and awaiting his *Uncle*, daydreaming about all the things he wants to do during the summer break.

There's an enormous bang, as a car backfires and into view drives what Isaac can only describe as a clapped-out red and yellow charabanc with green leather seats.

It's Uncle Ebenezer. Mr Ebenezer Strangeman!

6
Gravity Falls!

Isaac's initial reaction is to thank his lucky stars that no one is around to view such a spectacle, but as the vehicle draws closer, he sees that it is far from dilapidated. Instead, it is superbly maintained and looks as new as the day it rolled off the factory floor nearly one hundred years ago!

This mammoth car, or rather *bus*-car stands eight feet tall, suspended on four splendid spoked and white-walled wheels. Its bright red running boards are raised eighteen inches off the floor to go up and over the wheels and provide a step most people need help to climb. The bright red metalwork runs into a platform which supports a beautiful curved and shaped golden yellow carcass, sporting six doors down each side, identified by red beading and modest chromed handles.

Inside, or at least what Isaac can see given its raised elevation, are finely upholstered buttoned and edged green leather three-seater sofas - six to accompany each set of doors and offering comfort, even *Pullman* would applaud. The centre front engine housing stands like a small stately home with Classical proportioned grille and pediment and supporting a polished golden *flying* dolphin. There are four headlights, two positioned either side of the engine, and two set further back either side of the main body. There is a split windscreen, and a black folding roof - open and housed discretely at the rear.

Isaac's mouth opens like a visit to the dentist, as he removes his spectacles to rub his eyes and check he's not dreaming.

The horn honks three times, inhaling and exhaling a deep sound more akin to a tuba than a car horn. The driver's door swings open and the smartest and most dapper man, Isaac has ever seen, climbs down. He stands six feet three with a long white moleskin overcoat, highly polished black leather knee-high boots and a large green tweed eight-panel flat cap. Clean shaven, but with long shoulder length ginger red hair, he wears a crisp white high-collared shirt with a yellow bow tie, and red velvet waistcoat and breeches.

Removing one of his black leather gloves, the man offers his hand and says in haiku,

"You must be Isaac.
I'm, Ebenezer Strangeman.
So, pleased to meet you!"

"Hello, Uncle Ebenezer," replies Isaac, shaking his uncle's hand, suddenly lost for words.

"So, what do you think
of fantastic, *La Dauphine?*
Regal Princess, yes?"

asks Uncle Ebenezer pointing to his car, again speaking in haiku, trying to put Isaac at ease. Isaac soon discovers that this is how Uncle Ebenezer speaks - always in haiku...a triple-lined Japanese verse of five, seven and five syllables, not necessarily rhyming!

Uncle Ebenezer assists Isaac with his trunk before helping him clamber up into the front seat. Isaac edges his way to the passenger side and searches for a seatbelt.

"I'm sorry, no belts!
Hold on tight and look out for
the sharp-eyed police!"

jokes Uncle Ebenezer, smiling at Isaac before putting La Dauphine in gear to begin the return journey. La Dauphine purrs like a contented cat, occasionally *backfiring* as if to say something important or to ensure no one has fallen asleep!

Isaac sits silently, slightly intimidated and nervous. Every so often, he glances at Uncle Ebenezer, thinking to himself, "He's definitely *one in a million!* Why haven't we met before?"

Uncle Ebenezer opens a small door in the dashboard and takes out a red and white striped paper bag. Sweets! He breaks the silence, offering some to Isaac and saying,

"Please do take a sweet.
They are apple-favoured fudge
made by my own hands!"

Isaac pops a piece of fudge into his mouth. The taste is amazing. It's paradise - the taste of Eden. Like Adam being enticed and seduced by Eve, he tastes the distinctive flavours of golden apple, followed by green apple and finishing with red apple, as his mouth is delicately massaged, and his taste buds are tickled with a desire for more.

"Mmm," Isaac groans in delight. "Can I have another? They're absolutely *apple-icious!*" he adds, not normally one to invent words.

"Sure, of course, you can!
Take two, three or even four.
There are many more!"

Isaac's manners fly out of the open top, landing somewhere in a forgotten layby. He takes six and slowly savours each segment, trying in vain to show restraint but failing dismally. He finishes them in no time at all but thinks it a step too far to ask for more.

He will have to encourage Uncle Ebenezer to make more, regularly, every day, throughout the summer holiday!

Isaac relaxes and is now open to conversation, beginning, "So, Uncle Ebenezer. How are we related?"

"By marriage, not birth.
Your father's Ma's first husband
...his sister's first child!"

outlines Uncle Ebenezer, encouraging Isaac to take another sweet after Isaac's unconvincing refusal!

"So, you're more of a *step-second cousin* than an *uncle*, Uncle Ebenezer?" clarifies Isaac, giving Uncle Ebenezer a reassuring smile before prodding a little deeper, "Why haven't we met before?"

"Your father and I
never played when we were small.
Distant relatives!

My uncle estranged,
our worlds apart, once forgot,
ne'er the twain shall meet!"

finishes Uncle Ebenezer as if there's nothing more to add.

"But why now? How come my parents asked you to look after me now?" asks Isaac, realising that his question sounds disrespectful.

"Your parents alone
with no one else. Recalled me
from your Grandma's will!"

simply states Uncle Ebenezer, hoping his answer will satisfy Isaac.

"I'm glad!" reassures Isaac, desperately wanting to get off on the right foot, "I didn't think I had any family, apart from *Mother* and *Father* of course, and now I have you!"

Nothing more is said. La Dauphine carries Uncle Ebenezer and Isaac back to Uncle Ebenezer's home - somewhere Isaac hopes he can now call home...at least for the summer!

The best part of three hours passes. Isaac determines from the road signs that he is in the heart of Lincolnshire, somewhere north of Peterborough heading for Lincoln, and approaching a town called Grantham. South of Grantham, and just after a village named Colsterworth, Uncle Ebenezer turns right. The roads become narrow and overhung with trees on both sides as if tunnelling towards Uncle Ebenezer's home. Isaac focuses on the light at the end of the tunnel, but *blink, and you'll miss it*, Uncle Ebenezer turns left into a small opening in the leafy roadside wall.

There is a gated entrance with substantial pillars either side, both acting as plinths for stone carved *flying dolphins*. The gates are ornate black cast iron and *closed*. Uncle Ebenezer pretends to open them by shouting,

"No door should remain
unopen when those inside
seek love and friendship!"

Isaac is convinced Uncle Ebenezer presses a remote-controlled key, but he can't be one hundred per cent sure! He spies a black nameplate on the left-hand pillar with a white-topped embossing of *Gravity Falls* in a swirling font.

Isaac watches the gates close automatically and gets the same feeling of privacy when he locks the school lavatory door!

Creeping slowly up the winding drive, Isaac becomes aware of walled gardens, endless woods and an array of variously sized outhouses, some basic and functional, others more decorative and finished. There are pruned privets and life-size statues in every direction.

La Dauphine sweeps into the front courtyard, circling the central fountain, grand and spectacular with spouting waters and an enormous flying dolphin, cast in polished bronze and sparkling in the sunshine. Uncle Ebenezer stops the car and applies the handbrake, proclaiming,

"Welcome, Isaac, to
Gravity Falls. This is home,
and *what's mine is yours!*"

"Thank you, Uncle Ebenezer," responds Isaac, admiring the fountain, "Why *Gravity Falls*...is it because of the fountain?"

"Gravity Falls is
a wooded waterfall, and
more than meets the eye!"

Isaac is confused by the answer but interprets it as *eccentricity*. They collect Isaac's trunk and open the front door. Its exaggerated size creeks on oil-starved hinges and opens into an impressive hallway, diagonally tiled in large black and white marble and lit by an immense chandelier with lit crystals *falling* from the ceiling like a cascading waterfall - Gravity Falls!

Then unannounced, in bounds a *horse!* The greatest Great Dane Isaac has ever seen with a shiny black coat and size fourteen paws! The *Deutsche Dogge* halts when Uncle Ebenezer *wolf* whistles, standing as tall as Isaac and staring eye-to-eye. Uncle Ebenezer apologises,

"I forgot to say -
I hope you like dogs! This is
mine. Copernicus!"

"But when you say, *dog*," winces Isaac, smelling Copernicus's *dog breath* before joking, "you don't mean a miniature poodle!"

"He may be large, but
don't be afraid. He's just a
big softy at heart!"

reassures Uncle Ebenezer, cuddling Copernicus.

Isaac follows Uncle Ebenezer upstairs, observing how similar it is to Endeavours - every room individually named and resembling a dormitory. Uncle Ebenezer points left and right like an in-flight attendant identifying the exits before take-off, detailing,

"This is the Hall of
Visionaries. Go left for
science, right for *art!*

No two are the same -
all unique. Just take your pick
and feel free to change!

This room is mine, named
LE DAUPHIN. It's close at hand
in case you need me!"

Uncle Ebenezer gestures to the large central room behind him. Isaac saunters up and down both landings, observing an eclectic list of names, finally deciding on something familiar, "I think this one, Uncle Ebenezer," he says, leading Uncle Ebenezer down the left-hand landing and pointing to the last door on the right, *"ISAAC NEWTON!"*

Uncle Ebenezer nods his approval as he opens the door, adding,

"Now acquainted, no
more, *Uncle Ebenezer!*
Simply, *Ezer*, please!"

"Sure thing, Ezer!" answers Isaac, "Sure thing!"

7
Ker*fluffle*!

Ezer leads Isaac into the darkened room and places the trunk on the floor. Isaac fumbles for a light switch only to hear Ezer clap three times like the *toque de palmas* of a flamenco dancer. The room illuminates. It's not brightly lit, only in specific areas as if by candlelight.

Nightfall is descending fast.

It suddenly dawns on Isaac that he is standing in a room harking back to the seventeenth century - perhaps the original room of Isaac Newton! As he starts to his right and sweeps around the room, he spies a chest-high set of wooden drawers by the door, housing one, two, three, four, five, six full-width drawers. On the right-side wall is a floor to ceiling bookcase, complete and laden with facts and knowledge. Then a modest simply carved stone lintel fireplace with a gilt-framed mirror hanging directly above. Next to the fireplace is a substantial plan chest with large green leather-bound books stacked on top, and a series of hand drawn notes and working drawings held captive behind leather straps running diagonally across a wall hung noticeboard similar in size to the plan chest.

Then by the rear-facing window, incidentally with left and right red velvet curtains, is a three-quarter high wooden desk and an accompanying wooden high chair, and what appears to be quills, ink and parchment paper. Moving left freestands a blackboard with mathematical equations seemingly scribbled haphazardly in white chalk and headed *Law Three*. Isaac glances to the far-left corner, expecting to see just that, but observes a circular turret and spiral staircase winding its way to the ceiling like a string of DNA. Then there is a side-facing bay window with a red velvet upholstered full window seat, looking onto an orchard of regimented trees in full bloom, stretching some way back and enclosed within a high stone wall. The window has wooden folding panel shutters instead of curtains. The back wall has a simple hand basin and jug, next to a four-poster bed draped at the wall with rolling golden yellow fabric, matching the bedspread. Isaac completes his three-sixty tour observing a modest wooden bedside table and apple green coloured walls.

Isaac doesn't know where to begin!

Ezer smiles at Isaac's amazement, suggesting,

"Put your clothes in here,
and your trunk on top. Then meet
downstairs for dinner!"

"But where does the spiral staircase lead?" asks Isaac as his head begins to fill with endless questions.

"That's for me to know,
and you to find out! You will
thank your lucky stars!"

teases Ezer, laughing at Isaac and making his way to the door.

"And the orchard," begins Isaac, heading for the window and looking out over the dusk-lit trees, "are they apples?"

"Apples, pears and plums!
Centuries old, their fruits are
as sweet as heaven!"

replies Ezer, inadvertently licking his lips.

"How do you mean?" enquires Isaac.

"During Civil War,
Newton ran from home and hid
here...when just one tree!"

"Which tree?" asks Isaac, searching the orchard.

"That tree there, standing
tall, the only tree to bare
three distinctive fruits!

Not green or red or
golden, but all three...it's true!
Go see for yourself!

From that tree, apples
fell. To begin him thinking
about gravity!"

"You're kidding!" declares Isaac, wondering whether Ezer is leading him down the garden path.

"I kid you not, but
know others make claims elsewhere!
I promise. Why lie?

You've tasted my fudge
- wanted more! That's our secret
never to be told!

Now that's enough, I'm
hungry and so you must be!
Let's both head downstairs!"

"Sorry, Ezer!" apologises Isaac, following Ezer downstairs, "Your house is amazing. So much to see and so many questions to ask!"

Isaac follows Ezer into the kitchen, discussing dinner options and agreeing on *boiled egg and soldiers!*

Isaac stops in his tracks. It's like walking into a professional restaurant kitchen - *state of the art*, stainless steel and not a naked flame in sight. There are induction plates, Sous Vide baths, fryers, chillers, proving draws, convection ovens and extractors.

There are hands-free faucets, hanging utensils, preparation areas and high-tech gadgets, and everything is voice-controlled. Isaac thinks it's hilarious to hear Ezer *talk* to his kitchen, made funnier when the commands are in haiku!

Ezer disappears into a side room, returning inconceivably quickly, now dressed in a black chef's jacket, yellow and green checked chef's trousers, black plastic shoes and a red bandana tied around his ponytailed ginger red hair. Ezer is also wearing thick black rimmed glasses, and turns to Isaac, saying,

"Cooking is both *art*
and *science!* Yes, it's food, but
it is so much more!

Watch, and you will learn.
I will deconstruct boiled egg
...tastier than *good!*"

Isaac pulls himself up onto a black and chrome stool to see Ezer perform miracles. *Boiled egg and soldiers* to Isaac is a de-topped five-minute boiled egg in its shell, placed on an egg cup and served with a round of buttered toast cut into four or five pieces. *Boiled egg and soldiers* to *Chef Strangeman* is something completely different!

Isaac watches with intensity as Ezer takes two identical seventy-gram brown eggs freshly laid this morning onto special foam-filled nests by Mexican corn-fed French bantam free-range chickens. He breaks each uncooked egg, separating the *white* from the *yolk* into individual long rectangular dishes. He seasons the *white* with precisely measured Dead Sea salt and pestle and mortar cracked Indian pepper, and he adds a single one-centimetre cube of unsalted butter. This butter is freshly churned from Limousin cow's milk collected from three-year-old cows only grazed on French Limousin pastures above one thousand metres and is couriered and delivered earlier today!

Ezer heats the mixture to precisely fifty-five degrees Celsius, stirring with a special utensil until the butter and salt melts and fuses to create a rich translucent colour, speckled evenly with black pepper.

From a batch tin loaf, he made fresh today from North American wheat which he finely ground into flour using diamond dust-covered grinding plates, Ezer cuts two slices exactly fourteen millimetres thick using a special single slice cutting machine. Then each slice has all its crusts removed and is then divided into five equal strips measuring exactly thirty-three millimetres wide.

Ezer lays each strip into the *white* mixture and fully coats them before placing five strips per person onto a small square griddle pan.

Before placing the griddle pan in an oven, preheated to four hundred degrees Celsius, Ezer drops each egg yolk into a ceramic clamshell pot. These pots are shallow hinged egg coddlers, holding the perfect golden *pebbles* like an oyster holds its pearl.

Simultaneously, Ezer places one griddle into the oven and one clamshell into a steam chamber, repeating for both sets. Then he shouts,

"Two hundred and nine
seconds. Not a second less
nor a *second* more!"

Meanwhile, Ezer removes two specially designed cast iron serving plates from the plate warmer, again heated to exactly fifty-five degrees Celsius. The plates have two circular *clamshell* indents and five *soldier* indents and rest on English oak boards.

The kitchen timer doesn't ring or beep. It simply says in French, *"C'est l'heure, Chef. C'est l'heure!"* and automatically lowers the oven and steam chamber doors.

Ezer takes out each griddle and clamshell in the order in which he inserted them and dishes out the contents onto the serving plates. He takes each plate to the dining room, giving Isaac a jolted head gesture to follow.

Isaac sits beside Ezer and stares at the phenomenon laid before him. To the right of each plate is a key. It is long and triangular in section and attached to a golden flying dolphin as if the dolphin is blowing it from its blowhole. Isaac copies Ezer and inserts the key into his clamshell and turns. The clamshell opens slowly to reveal a golden *sun*, illuminating his face in yellow like a buttercup twizzled beneath a person's chin. Working *outside-in*, Isaac takes a *soldier* and stabs the egg. There is no eruption. The egg politely parts as if to embrace the soldier, evenly coating it ready to be eaten.

Isaac opens his mouth and takes the first bite. Like the apple-flavoured fudge, his mouth is treated to an experience beyond all experiences, spoiling him forever! Every dip is consistently the same. There is no need for a spoon as the clamshell holds and dispenses equal amounts until the last bite draws the final drop.

"I never knew *boiled egg and soldiers* could taste so good!" remarks Isaac, rubbing his tongue around his mouth to savour every last bit, "You are a culinary wizard, Ezer!"

"If I can do this
to an egg, watch me work with
all ingredients!"

boasts Ezer, smiling smugly at Isaac - delighted that he has ignited Isaac's culinary passion.

"What do you do, Ezer?" asks Isaac, fascinated by Ezer's enigmatic demeanour. "...for a living...to afford everything?"

"I invented a
belly button de-fluffer
...called it *Kerfluffle!*"

replies Ezer, pursing his lips and raising his eyebrows.

"I know *Kerfluffle!*" remarks Isaac, nodding then shaking his head, "This may sound rude, Ezer, but aren't they just *tweezers!*"

"It is all about
great design and marketing.
Just look at Appel!"

"Wow!" proclaims Isaac, "And what do you do now?"

"My parents said, *I
can be whatever I want
to be!* So, I am!"

"Have you ever been married?" says Isaac, straight to the point and not beating around the bush!

"Never met the right
girl. Talking in haiku, they
say, *He's a strange man!*

He's a strange man. Me,
Ezer Strangeman, but that's cool!
I'm happy as me!

Doing whatever
I want or feel like doing.
Who knows the future...!?"

replies Ezer, petering off at the end as if drifting into thought. Isaac senses sadness and missed opportunities but dismisses this when Ezer turns and challenges him to a game of chess!

Like *Pavlov's dog*, Isaac checks his watch. He is anticipating a hand-rung bell and *"lights out!"* before remembering Mr Hummock is no longer in charge, Ezer is! Ezer, who treats him as an equal and makes him feel special. Ezer, his new-found family and friend!

"What a great idea!" responds Isaac, helping Ezer return the dinner plates to the kitchen, "But I must warn you, Ezer. I'm the school champion!"

Ezer rubs his hands and leads Isaac into the living room, saying,

"Wrong first move, Isaac!
Never underestimate
your opposition!"

Ezer disappears briefly, again returning in an inconceivably short time to change from chef's outfit into a grey lounge suit, smart green shirt with red, yellow-dotted tie and light tan *Brogues*. On closer inspection, the yellow spots are flying dolphins.

Ezer and Isaac arrange their chess pieces. Isaac is *black,* and Ezer is *white*. As Ezer reaches into his trouser pocket for a coin to decide *who goes first*, he looks at Isaac and says,

"Do you like my suit?
I wore this last time I played
The World Chess Master!"

"And who won?" asks Isaac, realising that *school champion* doesn't sound so good anymore! Repeating, "Who won, Ezer?"

Ezer says nothing. He knows this will rock Isaac's boat.

Sometimes silence is more powerful than words!

8

Apple pie!

Isaac and Ezer play three games of chess - two are hard fought, but the first is embarrassingly short as Ezer suckers Isaac into a schoolboy error and beats him with his recipe of attack - playing the *Queen's Gambit* and checkmating Isaac in seven moves!

"You play a good game,
but I, *Le Dauphin* - always
defend King and Queen!"

declares Ezer, inhaling deeply before exhaling with contentment at thrashing Isaac three to nothing, adding,

"One only improves
if one is truly tested...
never handed a win!"

"I totally agree," replies Isaac, helping Ezer to reset the chessboard, joking, "but did you have to be so ruthless!?"

Isaac and Ezer give each other a knowing glance and agree to play every day. Isaac bids Ezer goodnight and makes his way upstairs. He is tired but intrigued to discover what lies at the top of his spiral stairs.

"Goodnight, Ezer," declares Isaac, stifling a yawn, "It's so nice to meet you and thank you for everything."

"Think nothing of it!
See you bright and early in
the morning. Goodnight!"

replies Ezer, raising his hand to gesture Isaac like a native American saying *how* then reaching for a book when Isaac leaves the room.

Copernicus stirs as Isaac wanders through the front hall and accompanies him upstairs as if to chaperon and deliver him safely to his room. Isaac opens his door, claps three times to turn on the lights then orders Copernicus downstairs.

He gazes out of both windows, staring into unchartered territory at the rear of the house before watching the moon shimmer on the orchard trees as if they are reflecting the starlit sky above.

Reaching the spiral staircase, Isaac grabs hold of the wooden bannister, noting its well-worn smoothness. He claps three times to illuminate the stairs only to turn out the room lights...completely! It makes him snigger, and he tries all possible combinations under the sun before satisfying himself that the room only has one setting - three claps for on or off and nothing in between. As he intuitively winds his way up the conventional *tread to riser* proportions, he realises why no additional light is necessary. Like an on-duty meerkat raising its head above the parapet, he pokes his head through the ceiling floor to discover a domed room with two shutters, open to the night sky and allowing the moon to sprinkle highlights on the objects within.

There in the middle of the room, exactly centred and mounted on an enormous wooden spherical ball is a large wooden telescope angled and pointing directly to the open shutters. With his knowledge, gained as a member of the school astronomy club, Isaac recognises it as a Newtonian reflecting telescope. It is similar to the one at school, but this one is made from polished wood and turned brass with a perpendicular side-mounted viewing eyepiece and a simple mechanism for adjusting the focal length. Isaac is intrigued to know if it is Isaac Newton's telescope or merely a replica...he will ask Ezer in the morning.

Isaac walks around the telescope in stunned amazement and excitement. The multi-directional wooden sphere, which Isaac estimates to be over a foot in diameter, is mounted by a metal bracket to a wooden spindle connecting to a large wooden circular floor-mounted plinth. Around this spindle is a horizontal spoked wheel identical in detail to an old ship's wheel with eight wood-turned handles equally spaced around the outside. On the floor is a large circular disc which Isaac believes is a standing platform, encircled with a three-foot-high metal railing and three metal rods, extending outwards and attaching to a central metal ring running around the entirety of the domed room.

On the railing, directly opposite the shutters, Isaac notices a latch and some runners. He makes his way around, limboing under one of the extending wall rods and lifts the latch. The gate revolves open. Isaac steps onto the circular floor and closes the gate behind him. He walks over to the eyepiece and finds a set of wooden steps spiralling around a five-foot ornate wooden pole fixed to the floor. The steps are designed to revolve around the pole to provide the correct step height and position for comfortable telescope viewing - in Isaac's case, the third and top step. So simple and so clever thinks Isaac as he adjusts and climbs up the steps.

Isaac finds a handwritten note attached to the eyepiece. It's from Ezer and reads,

"Isaac. Look to the
stars and beyond - starting with
The Flying Dolphin!"

Isaac is a little confused. He detaches the note and pivots his spectacles around his ears until they nest neatly on the crown of his head. Closing his left eye, he places his right eye on the eyepiece, rotating the sight adjuster until the blurred image comes into focus. Isaac pulls away in astonishment, shaking his head and rubbing his right eye in disbelief. He looks again and declares, "OMG!"

Glistening in the night sky is a constellation Isaac has never seen. Like a child joining a dot to dot picture by numbers, he identifies two tail *flukes*, then a dorsal fin, then a pronounced *melon* head and a *rostrum* snout, then an underbelly with a single flipper and then back to the tail. The Flying Dolphin!

Isaac marvels at this for some time before repositioning the telescope on its *ball and socket* mounting. As he adjusts the focal length, he spies Saturn or at least half of it - the other half hiding behind the right shutter. The opening isn't wide enough, but It suddenly occurs to him why there is a horizontal wheel. He grabs one of the spigot handles and pulls it towards him. There is a creaking noise beneath the standing platform as the gears engage and begin turning. Isaac feels the platform moving together with the whole domed roof and its windowed section. Although the engineering is rather crude, there is an underlying precision where one full turn of the wheel moves the dome, the telescope and Isaac by one degree. Isaac turns the wheel fifteen times before revisiting Saturn, now in full view and distinctive in its ringed magnificence.

Time passes in the blink of an eye...Isaac's right eye...as he spends the next hour taking a three-sixty tour of space, observing the moon, shooting stars, well-known constellations and even The International Space Station. The image is so crystal clear, Isaac convinces himself he sees an astronaut staring back!

Isaac finds The Flying Dolphin again and decides to call it a day, retracing his steps down the spiral staircase and into his room.

Pouring water from the large jug into the even larger ceramic bowl, Isaac grabs his toothbrush and begins preparing for bed. His trunk can wait until the morning - why end the day on a tedious task when he can finish on a high and take the most incredible last eight hours to bed with him.

Isaac pulls the golden yellow bedspread back to reveal two plump pillows and a crisp white sheet capping a red blanket which he flaps open. He inserts his legs and begins to stretch them only to find a *cul-de-sac!* Isaac leaps out of bed and pulls back the sheets to find another note from Ezer, and an *apple pie!*

"Got you, Isaac! Just
a little prank I thought you'd
appreciate! Night!"

Isaac is accustomed to an *apple pie* - when a single sheet is folded back to half its length and disguised to appear normal, but since duvets were introduced at Endeavours, they have become relegated to the past...or so he thought!

He remakes his bed, shaking his head and muttering under his breath, "Ezer...Ezer...Ezer funny man!"

Three claps and the lights are out, literally and figuratively.

Isaac wakes to the heat of the morning sun as it creeps through the side window and unleashes like a laser beam. Isaac forgot to close the curtains and shutters when he climbed into bed under the guise of midnight.

His first reaction is one of confusion and unfamiliarity until he remembers Ezer and ISAAC NEWTON. He jumps out of bed with unparalleled vigour for the new day, wondering what Ezer will have in store. Unlatching his trunk locks and throwing its tethered lid open, Isaac opens the chest of drawers fourth-from-bottom drawer, positioned at the most convenient height. He expects to see an empty void ready to fill with his belongings, but instead finds an array of different clothes and outfits. There are polo shirts, long and short sleeved T-shirts, various coloured dress shirts and yet another note from Ezer!

"We can't have you in
school uniform! These are yours.
Hope the sizes fit!"

Isaac opens the other drawers. The bottom two drawers are empty and available for his trunk items while the remaining three drawers have sports gear, cycling gear, wetsuits, swimming trunks, a chef's outfit, various jackets, blazers, socks, underwear, accessories including belts, ties and hats, and several pairs of shoes ranging from smart Brogues to flip-flops!

Isaac dresses in green combat style trousers, yellow baseball boots, and a red T-shirt with three white stars printed down each sleeve and one large white star printed on the front. He finishes it with a black linen cap and a stonewashed effect denim jacket, immediately turning up the collar for added *swagger!*

As he goes to leave, he notices an old red leather book on the lower shelf of his bedside table. He picks it up and studies the green edge-printed pages and golden title letters, displaying *Newton's Laws of Motion & Gravity* before thumbing through it and remarking to himself, "I suppose this is Ezer's idea of a little light bedtime reading!"

Every time Isaac attempts to read one of the laws, it soon stretches beyond his current understanding and knowledge. As he closes the book and goes to put it back, he spies a single sheet of paper. It's another note from Ezer. There is no joking this time. Instead, it reads,

"These simple notes will
help you understand Newton's
great Laws of Physics!

They are important
and fundamental to all
of life and beyond!

Three laws of motion
solidify the concepts
- Force, Mass, Inertia!

FIRST LAW OF MOTION.
An object will continue
to move straight and in

the same direction
at the same speed, or remain
in a state of rest

until a push or
pull *Force* acts on it. Motion
is changed. Inertia!

SECOND MOTION LAW.
It defines how big the push
or pull force needed

to accelerate
objects with *Mass* where *Mass* is
how big the object!

The *Force* in Newtons
equals *Acceleration* -
metres per second^2,

multiplied by *Mass* -
kilograms. Also expressed,
F equals *MA!*

THIRD LAW OF MOTION.
Every action has equal,
opposed reaction!

Force of object on
another object's the same,
but the other way!

Like balls striking or
rocket propulsion. If one's
Mass-ive...small effect!

LAW OF GRAVITY.
Gravity is a pull *Force*
between two *Masses!*

Greater *Force* if *Mass*
increases, lesser *Force* if
distance increases!

It's why objects fall
to ground and the moon does not
fly away from earth!"

Ezer ends with a simple summary,

"These laws put *man on
the moon*...Einstein's platform for
Relativity!

And if you're puzzled,
second² reads as...per second
every second!"

Isaac reads the page twice, thinking what a great teacher Ezer would make. Rather than put it back with the leather-bound book, he folds it in half then half again and places it in his jacket inside pocket. He wants to read it again and again until he memorises it off by heart.

9
The hall of visionaries!

Isaac closes his door. He is inquisitive to find out what lies behind the other bedroom doors, split so distinctly between *science* and *art*. Directly opposite is *CHARLES DARWIN.* Isaac turns the door handle and peers around the door as if visiting Mr Hill's office. The room resembles a ship's interior, possibly the captain's quarters of HMS Beagle Isaac presumes, curving in polished English oak towards the window that slopes backwards and is split into five gilt-framed and arch-topped sections, all glazed with fine metal muntins. The ceiling is also polished English oak with a gentle bow from side to side.

In front of the window is a large table with a single green leather swivel armchair at the far end. There is a large map laid out on the table with a route to *The Galapagos Islands* scribed in red ink. On the right wall runs a red covered single bed, made *private* by two green curtains framing left and right, presently tied-back with ornate yellow ropes.

There are scores of animals and various species housed under glass bell jars or inside glass-fronted cabinets, scattered haphazardly around the room and walls. A stuffed dodo exhibit takes centre stage. A first edition of *The Origin of Species* is displayed on a lectern and open to chapter fifteen, entitled *The Theory of Evolution* with a newspaper clipping acting as a bookmark - headed, *Darwin is doing for biology what Newton did for physics, and influencing the way people view the planet.*

As Isaac circles the room, he turns to view the back wall. It forces him to take one step backwards as he confronts a life-size painting of *The Evolution of Man*, charting ape to modern man in descending height and chronological order. It's both intimidating and impressive at the same time.

Isaac steadies himself on an exhibit, unsure if he's imagining the room swaying as if sailing the high seas, or whether it's just his reaction to witnessing such a rich setting.

There are no other adjoining rooms or spiral staircases, and no notes from Ezer! Isaac takes one last look at the room, standing beside The Evolution of Man, recalling Galileo's yellow flag. The painting is so lifelike - it's as if he can smell the individual body odours, and he immediately flash-backs to the Whitton Wash!

Isaac exits and moves to the next room on his right - *THOMAS EDISON*. He opens the door expecting to see an inventor's paradise - a laboratory of contraptions and experiments in various stages of development. Instead, Isaac finds a dark room - totally black as if walking into a photographic developing room.

Isaac searches unsuccessfully for a light switch. He opens the door further to see if this helps but realises that there is a black velvet semicircular curtain hanging around the entrance. He pats the curtain like a theatrical compere in search of an opening to the stage. Isaac finally gains access where the curtain meets the wall. The room is still pitch black, confusing Isaac. He claps three times. There is no light. Then he hears the faint sound of music, simplistically played on some form of early phonograph or gramophone. It increases in volume and accompanies a woman reciting the biblical verse,

"In the beginning, God created the heaven and the earth.

And the earth was without form and void, and darkness was upon the face of the deep. And the Spirit of God moved upon the face of the waters."

At the start of the third verse, a single incandescent light, hanging from the centre of the ceiling, begins to glow, becoming brighter with every word.

"And God said, let there be light, and there was light."

By the fourth and final verse, the lightbulb is fully illuminated and joins a spectacle of light, as hundreds of lights flash and strobe as if conducted by a mad wizard consumed by some greater power.

"And God saw the light, and it was good, and God divided the light from darkness."

Isaac can make out a simple bed, a wardrobe and a bedside table but they seem insignificant compared with the onslaught of light and sound on his senses. It is then that he comprehends the symbolism.

It is the genius of invention. Inventions that radically change the world - like the electric lightbulb and recorded sound...giving the power of instant light, and sound reproduction.

As the phrase repeats, the sound fades away, and the lights cease from flashing. They are replaced by the latest LED technology to create the illusion of daylight in this once darkened room.

Isaac looks to his left and there on the wall is an old-fashioned jukebox, standing cathedral-like and charismatic with red, green and yellow lights softly pulsating as if depicting inner life. Isaac walks over and peers into its *shop window*. Unexpectedly, there is an electronic display. It invitingly says, "You name it, Isaac and I'll play it!"

Before Isaac can think of his favourite tune, the jukebox proclaims rather robotically, "Let's get this party started! Let's rock to *School's Out for Summer* by AC/DC!"

The surround sound beats through Isaac like a string of heavyweight punches... but it's too early for heavy rock!

Isaac brings everything to an end, suddenly appreciating the context of AC and DC and Edison's plight between the two electrical variants. It makes him smile as he claps three times. Everything shuts down, and he exits through the black velvet curtain into the landing to see the room opposite - *MARIE CURIE*.

Isaac is conscious of time...and he's hungry, but his appetite has been *wet!*

Isaac opens the door. He is confronted by black and white. The left-hand side of the room is black, and the right-hand side of the room is white, divided through the bay window and the simple *queen* bed in front of it. The black half of the bay window has tinted dark glass while the white half is transparent. The bed's headboard is upholstered in half black, and half white material and the matching bedspread is half black and half white.

Isaac looks at the half black, half white tiled floor. On the black side, carefully painted in an iridescent paint and glowing green is the word *PHYSICS* and painted in gloss red paint on the white side, is the word *CHEMISTRY*. Nobel Prizes hang proud on both sides - the black side is further inscribed with *1906* and *the first woman*, and the white side is further inscribed with *1911* and *the first woman in two categories.*

Each side of the room also has a long laboratory bench with various machines and lab equipment. The black side has a wall-hung illuminated lightbox showing a *landscape* of X-rays. Isaac imagines they must be Marie Curie's skeleton. The white side has radioactive measuring equipment and a hanging periodic table, boldly marking elements *eighty-four* and *eighty-eight* - Polonium and Radium.

As Isaac turns to leave, he discovers, embroidered in yellow at the foot of the bedspread, *I am among those who think that science has great beauty.*

Walking across the landing and past Ezer's room, Isaac senses a definite change. The air feels lighter and the mood more relaxed. It makes him shudder and shake his shoulders as if pressing *refresh*.

On his first left is a room marked *COCO CHANEL*. Unlike the other rooms, it is double doored. The handles are two large letter C's, interlocking and crossed, and cleverly separated down the middle. Isaac grabs each chrome plated handle and makes a grand entrance as he swings open both doors simultaneously.

The first thing that hits him is the fragrance. Its smells like a walk in the park, the beach and the countryside combined! Then he's struck by the room's simplicity. The carpet and walls are cream-coloured with just a hint of green. There is a curved bay window with floor to ceiling vertical glazing - one, two, three, four, *five* panels in total. Directly in front of the window is a concentric circular bed tailored in a deep red cashmere cover, accented with gold taffeta round cushions. Above the bed is an identical sized circular light fitting, beaming like a large sun. On further inspection, Isaac sees that it's a glass skylight, open to starlit evenings and sunlit days.

Down each side of the room is floor to ceiling, vertical mirrors, seamless and flush, again five on each side. Isaac uses his right shoulder to see if the mirror panels open. Sure enough, a panel opens as if by magic to reveal rows of clothes, clearly marked by year and with accompanying handbag and jewellery accessories. Isaac promises to explore the other panels one rainy day!

Closing the panel and trying not to mark the mirrored glass, Isaac turns to see two mannequins simply posed either side of the grand doors. One is dressed in an elegant black suit with a blue and white horizontal striped sailor's top - masculine in concept but undeniably feminine in its implementation. The other is wearing a classic *little black dress* - timeless and designed to complement both a woman's figure and her modern lifestyle.

Exiting *COCO CHANEL*, Isaac walks straight over to *WILLIAM SHAKESPEARE*. It's not what Isaac was imagining!

It feels more like a trip to the dentist than some theatre or playhouse. The room is pure white - floor, ceiling and walls, and the window has a translucent white screen applied to it, equalising the light and giving the whole room a Zenlike glow. There are no wardrobes or chest of drawers, just a single white bookcase with the *Complete Works of Shakespeare* displayed for inspiration, divided into red leather-bound *tragedies*, green leather-bound *romances*, yellow leather-bound *comedies* and black leather-bound *sonnets*. In the centre of the room is what Isaac can only describe as a dentist's chair, standing in isolation like a medieval torture device! It is white and self-adjusts from sitting to fully reclined, has a downlight for best reading conditions, and an articulating electronic screen to provide the most comfortable reading angle. It explains the lack of bed!

"Wow!" remarks Isaac as he retreats backwards, closing the door, "This is unquestionably for those who want to *eat, sleep and breathe* Shakespeare!" adding with a wry smile, "Perhaps these *tales* are better suited to *winter* than a *midsummer's night!*"

Venturing to the end of the landing, Isaac opts for the left-hand room - *FRANK LLOYD WRIGHT*...interested to see how it compares as a mirror-image of *ISAAC NEWTON*. He pushes the recessed handle, but to no avail - the door slides. With the most delicate of touches, Isaac moves the door into its frame, watching it magically return when he steps inside.

Instead of a chimney, there is a large superior-sized white linen bed, standing elephant-like on four corner circular columns. Isaac can hear running water. Searching the room, he sees that the wall behind the bed has a clear flush panel covering water cascading from the ceiling. The ceiling appears to float - spaced away from the wall with a two-inch groove. As the water runs down a stainless-steel backdrop, it runs under the bed and out towards the right wall. Isaac walks to the front of the bed to find a clear floor section with water running over rocks and gravel, rippling softly as if playing the keys of a virtuoso's piano. The room invisibly cantilevers beyond the house exterior like a modern Juliet balcony but searching for countryside rather than some solitary Romeo! Isaac watches the water fall down the side of the house and into a tranquil water feature - carefully crafted and considered in the landscaped garden below.

Isaac then spies a similar turret in the corner of the room. The spiral staircase is not centrally positioned. Instead, it hugs the walls, is made from solid concrete and has no steps. Isaac walks up the spiralling ramp, admiring works of art and strategically positioned window openings before spotting that there is no domed roof or telescope at the top. The flat ceiling is glazed with an ever decreasing spiral muntin - hypnotic and giving the illusion of stretching *ad infinitum*. It is *functional beauty*.

Retracing his steps, Isaac notes a long horizontal frameless window on the rear-side wall showing a similar garden view to his room. To the right of the bed appear to be flush wardrobes or an ensuite bathroom, but Isaac is eager to see the last room.

He opens the door to *JOHN LENNON*. The whole right-side wall is *tiled* in butting black frames with glistening gold, platinum and diamond discs, incidentally paying homage to Thomas Edison. Isaac counts eight high and fifteen long, totalling one hundred and twenty. Most read, *Lennon-McCartney*, some just, *Lennon*. There is a random white sack lying on the floor. Guitars are hanging on the front wall to the right of the bed - acoustic and electric types in various colours and finishes. A black suit hangs over a chair and beneath rests a pair of *Winklepickers*. There is a simple white double bed sunk into a floor-mounted white plinth. The white painted metal window lies directly behind the bed and spans floor to ceiling in four divisions. On the window are two hand-drawn messages. One says *LOVE,* and the other says *PEACE*. To the left of the bed and positioned in front of the side-facing window sits a large white grand piano - keys locked...a copy of *The Catcher in the Rye*, lying nonchalantly on top.

As Isaac leaves, he stops to stare at a gigantic green apple painted on the back wall. It is food for thought. He gazes to the ceiling in contemplation to discover, much to his continuing amazement, the hand-drawn inscription...*IMAGINE*...

10
One Newton apple!

Isaac makes his way downstairs. He can't work out if viewing the other rooms has satisfied his curiosity or only acted to ignite an inner fire or drown him in a thirst for knowledge. He's happy with his room choice, but would he feel as at home in another? It makes him think. Where does his future lie? Which landing will entice him most? He shakes his head dismissively. There is no need to burden himself with such concerns or build on his dream as a five-year-old of becoming a fireman or a tap dancer!

Copernicus is a happy distraction as he greets Isaac at the bottom of the stairs, barging into him like an American football running back in search of the end zone. They walk together into the kitchen. There is no Ezer - only the seductive and lingering smells of the recently prepared breakfast. Isaac is pulled towards the dining room by the sound of music like some dirty rat following the *Pied Piper's* flute. He wanders through, and sure enough there sits Ezer in some *Bohemian Rhapsody!* His arms are outstretched, and his head points *heavenwards* as the inimitable and mercurial singer screams, *"Thunderbolt and lightning, very, very frightening. Galileo, Galileo!"*

Nothing surprises Isaac anymore. Ezer claps twice to interrupt the song, turning to Isaac with a hint of embarrassment and saying,

"Good morning, Isaac!
You can't beat a bit of *Queen*
to start the new day!"

Isaac sits down beside Ezer, immediately salivating as he spies the creative concoction laid before him, and Ezer declaring,

"A sausage sandwich
like you've never tasted! Get
your chops around it!

What would you like to
drink? A cup of tea or my
Chocolate Surprise?"

"It has to be your Chocolate Surprise!" says Isaac, wondering how best to tackle the perfect square sandwich - helped by the lack of cutlery, "What is your Chocolate Surprise?"

"If I told you then
It wouldn't be a surprise!
I'll be back in five..."

replies Ezer, disappearing to begin another conversation with his kitchen!

Isaac grabs the sandwich with both hands and lifts it to his mouth. The outer bread is toasted with an equal golden colour on all sides - any sort of join is invisible and perplexing. There are no crusts. With no airs and graces, Isaac takes a big bite from the centre. The familiar sausage flavour introduces itself before welcoming the perfect balance of seasoning and brown sauce, improved with a smidgeon of English mustard. Then there is a flashback of fudge as Isaac tastes the distinctive flavour of golden apple, infused and precisely cut into crisp three-millimetre cubes. He studies the sandwich. There is a five-pointed star cross-section sausage with a central core housing what Isaac assumes is the sauce and seasoning. Isaac bites the left corner to taste red apple flavoured sausage, and then he bites the right corner to taste green apple flavoured sausage.

Ezer is right - it is sausage heaven. Not even Arthur's *E-day* sausage comes close as Isaac finds it impossible to choose which bite to take next from the three-star sausage selection, although it would be *five stars* if he were asked to rate it. He tries to savour every mouthful, but it's as if he's never tasted *food* before, devouring the remaining sandwich in seconds like a young child with a forbidden cake.

Ezer returns carrying two mug-sized *golden droplets* - highly polished and beautifully crafted. Both are engraved with a flying dolphin. Placing one in front of Isaac, Ezer sits down, explaining,

"Grip it with both hands,
and turn upside down. Place the
end into your mouth.

Press the button on
top and let gravity do
the rest. Just watch me!"

Isaac copies Ezer and tastes the sweetest and yet most bitter chocolate he has ever sampled. It glides down his throat, appearing to disengage his swallowing reflex - heated to body temperature and melting as if supplying a life-giving blood transfusion. Then there is a hint of apple. Surprise! Red apple follows golden apple follows green apple, all enhanced and aerated by the clever valve system. Just as Isaac thinks he can take no more, it finishes. Not too much, not too little - just the right amount!

Ezer and Isaac put the golden droplets back on the table. Ezer looks at Isaac and unexpectedly, excluding all decorum, burps the biggest burp, Isaac has ever heard! Isaac bursts into laughter, but within seconds, he too lets out the biggest burp he's ever burped, reliving the Chocolate Surprise once more!

It is the best breakfast - a sausage sandwich to die for and a Chocolate Surprise to leave Isaac not only astounded but the most content he's ever felt.

"I looked in at all the other rooms, Ezer," begins Isaac, hoping this is acceptable, "WOW! What an amazing and completely contrasting set they are!"

"It's a funny thing.
Who to include...who to
exclude. Difficult!
BEETHOVEN before
LENNON - t'was a case of *roll
over BEETHOVEN!*
Thinking to replace
LLOYD WRIGHT with ZAHA HADID,
and STEPHEN HAWKING
to replace NEWTON.
MCQUEEN or YVES SAINT LAURENT
to replace CHANEL.
Replace EDISON
- STEVE JOBS or ALAN TURING?
It's so personal!
The only rule I
set is - they must be deceased
...with a legacy!"

informs Ezer, delighted to share his list of visionaries with Isaac, delighted to share his list with someone who appreciates.

"I love that every room personifies them while making a statement or inciting interpretation," compliments Isaac, commenting further, "I like them all and can't wait to revisit them over the holiday, but the one that stands out most is JOHN LENNON!"

"A pop star with an
idealistic dream. Seen
wrongly as a threat

because he dared to
question the status quo and
want a better life!"

responds Ezer, falling into a Liverpudlian accent and *flattening* his
nose for added effect.

"The room felt like it asked more questions than it answered,"
continues Isaac, unsure what he means but is comforted to see
Ezer nodding in agreement and answering,

"A life cut short. Shot
by a lunatic just as
he felt normalcy!

Who knows what he could
have done - what future greatness
he would have achieved!

Imagine if John
Lennon wasn't shot. Imagine
just what could have been!"

And with that, Ezer requests in haiku the song, *Imagine* as if
unlocking the keys on the white grand piano in JOHN LENNON
and continuing the legacy of questioning and provocation. As the
song ends to, *"And the world will be as one."* Ezer turns to Isaac
and says,

"Right, young man! How do
you fancy a bike ride? To
see around the grounds..."

"Sounds fantastic!" replies Isaac, helping Ezer return the plates
and *droplets* to the kitchen, "I haven't been on a bike in ages. No
one has a bike at school, strange as it may sound!"

"I suggest you change.
You'll find suitable attire
In your bedroom chest!"

instructs Ezer, walking Isaac through to the hall and upstairs, agreeing to meet by the front door in five minutes.

"Oh, by the way," says Isaac, as Ezer opens his door to LE DAUPHIN, "Is the telescope an original Newtonian or a replica?"

"It is original.
The very telescope he
invented and used!"

informs Ezer, turning and closing his door - unaware of Isaac's look of disbelief. Isaac walks back to his room, overexcited at the thought of using the same telescope as Isaac Newton - looking through the same eyepiece and observing the same stars and beyond.

Isaac meets Ezer by the front door. They are both clad in lycra cycle suits. Ezer's is bright red with a yellow stripe running down each side. Isaac's is bright green, again with a yellow stripe running down each side. Both have a yellow flying dolphin printed on the back.

Ezer leads Isaac out of the front door and to the right, suggesting he shows Isaac the orchard en route to the bicycle shed. They come to the enclosed wall, partially disguised with climbing roses, full blooming in red and yellow flowers and complementing the rich green foliage. Ezer opens a large round-arched wooden gate, painted in charcoal grey to match the grey stonework.

It's like walking into a platoon of soldiers on parade, each tree spaced equally apart from the next, standing to attention in dress uniform - its leaves neatly and carefully pruned...the fruit polished and glowing as if ready for inspection. There are three columns and one, two, three, four, five, six, seven rows, counts Isaac, totalling twenty-one. Ezer points to a column of pears, a column of apples and a column of pears. The plums are purple and plump. The pears are bulbous and bulging. The apples are round and rotund.

The smell is stupendous and scintillatingly delectable! Bees buzz around the border flowers. They are teased and tempted by bright colours and *magic* stamen, promising *buckets* of nectar in exchange for cross-pollination. Wasps hover around the tree fruit, enticed by the aroma but they are no match for the thick and ripening skins. Butterflies fly majestically everywhere, fluttering silently in the cool morning breeze. The occasional dragonfly darts through the orchard...more by luck than design. Birds chirp and call out from the higher branches, resting after an early morning start collecting fresh, rich pickings and delicacies of worms, grubs and pupae.

Isaac walks along the apple tree column, past a golden apple tree, then a green apple tree and then a red apple tree until he reaches the middle orchard tree - taller, older and with greater girth. It is Isaac Newton's tree, laden with all three colour apple types and standing like a force to be reckoned with - the other trees seemingly attracted and gravitating to its central core.

Ezer squeezes one of the red Newton apples to test its near perfect ripeness then educates Isaac,

"They ripen early
and are the same, weighing one
hundred and two grams!"

"How's that?" enquires Isaac, dumbfounded by this rare regularity in nature.

"The *Force* in Newtons
equals *Acceleration* -
metres per second^2,

multiplied by *Mass* -
kilograms. Also expressed,
F equals *MA!*

One Newton is the
accelerating force of
one-kilogram *Mass*.

Newton calculates
gravity at nine point eight
metres per second^2.

So, *a One Newton
Apple* weighs one hundred and
two grams exactly!"

concludes Ezer, hoping that Isaac understands...tempted to repeat his explanation.

"This is amazing!" declares Isaac, "Newton's tree not only has three different colour apple types but is also the bearer of the exact size apple for his calculation of a one Newton force!"

"And please don't forget
their amazing taste. The taste
of heaven on earth!"

reminds Ezer, smiling fondly at Isaac.

"Of course, Ezer!" agrees Isaac, smiling back, "How can I forget their amazing taste!"

11
Our friend's electric!

Isaac and Ezer leave the orchard through the rear gate, chatting about Newton's apples and all the things they are going to cook during the holiday. Isaac repeats his fudge request several times but fears he's in danger of over-egging it!

Isaac gets his first real glimpse of the rear garden, ordinary and straightforward close to the house with a formal stone patio and a manicured lawn. However, there is a strange looking conical structure directly below Ezer's bedroom, half in the patio and half in the lawn. Isaac estimates it to be about twenty feet in diameter and made of copper. Its peak is silver and topped with a golden flying dolphin.

"What's that?" asks Isaac, pointing to the bizarre structure. Ezer says nothing. Instead, he claps three times. Isaac recognises a different rhythm with Ezer's claps. This set has a long first clap followed by two short claps, almost *Morse code* in its simplicity.

The cone lifts automatically on three telescopic pillars like a UFO, appearing to hover before it raises seven feet above the ground to reveal a circular three-foot high stone wall. Inside the wall are a central circular dining table and chairs with more comfortable seating running around the wall circumference, including Romanesque loungers and enormous beanbags. There is a cooking area at the lawn end with what appears to be the outside equivalent of Ezer's kitchen albeit compact and geared to outside cooking.

"OMG!" remarks Isaac, "How cool is that!"

"Let's eat alfresco
tonight, Isaac. Nothing like
cooking food outside!"

suggests Ezer, clapping three times in reverse to close the cone.

As Isaac's eyes make their way up the gently rising garden, it becomes apparent that the garden is an impressive triangular plot, drawing the eye passed tree-lined converging sides to a distant point - a circular domed stone *folly* with a terraced water feature, radially stepping down three tiers to the lawn. The water reflects the bright green grass, rippling and shimmering in the light and animating the lawn. On top of the folly is a golden flying dolphin. The garden's geometric simplicity certainly focuses the mind and is inherently calming and spiritual.

Isaac and Ezer head for an angled stone wall at the bottom left apex and walk through a large open arch.

Isaac imagines the bike shed to be a modest structure, possibly a wooden garden shed - its main purpose to protect the bikes from the weather and keep them secure from any uninvited light-fingers. He couldn't be more wrong!

There is a parallelogram enclosed courtyard with similar arched openings on three sides. The flooring resembles a chessboard but with alternate light and dark stone parallelogram-shaped paving slabs. On the opposite side is a long building stretching at least one hundred feet left to right. There is a substantial double doored wooden entrance to the left side, and a long uninterrupted glazed window ranged off the door's top edge, going halfway down and running the entire length of the building.

"This is my workshop -
where I invent, tinker and
house my possessions!"

describes Ezer, leading Isaac to the front door and opening a smaller door in the right-hand leaf.

"It's more like a supermarket!" remarks Isaac, impressed with the square footage and the array of *goodies* on show. "Oh, look. There's La Dauphine!" adds Isaac, pointing to the far end.

It's like walking into an Aladdin's cave if gadgets, weird and wonderful vehicles and crazy collectables are your treasure! And there are 3D printers, lathes, milling machines and endless engineering and workshop tools, systematically ordered and hung on dedicated wall cut-outs. A circular spray booth stands alone, creating a floor to ceiling column and disguising any ventilation outlet - its transparent swivelling door revealing Ezer's latest project...something that looks like an extra-terrestrial golden flying saucer!

"What's that, Ezer?" enquires Isaac, pointing to the spray booth.

"A bespoke golf cart
to assemble with glass roof
and hidden chassis!"

replies Ezer, showing Isaac the modified equilateral triangular three-wheel chassis and a ceiling mounted pulley system holding a large domed clear glass roof. The roof appears to have a clever rear hinge assembly with cantilevers to spread the force and help to open and close the dome with more control.

"Why only three wheels?" enquires Isaac, examining the electric chassis and moving the steering wheel left and right.

"Like a motor trike -
two stable rear wheels and front
central steering wheel.

Single driver and
room for two passengers next
to each rear wheel hub!"

"Where are the seats?" asks Isaac, keen to see the interior.

Ezer goes to a bench running along the front window and pulls a white sheet as if unveiling a menacing ghost to reveal three identical single seats. They look more like racing seats than any seat you would associate with a golf cart. One rear seat is upholstered in green leather, another in yellow leather while the front seat is upholstered in red leather, all three with matched edge piping.

"They're gorgeous," declares Isaac, running his hand over the brand-new leather and feeling the soft padding contained within. "And the engine, or rather motor...where's that?"

"I am picking the
souped-up motor tomorrow
from the specialists.

So, Isaac, you'll be
alone until I return
...around eleven!"

informs Ezer with a look of excitement like that of a child on Christmas Eve!

"No problem, Ezer," responds Isaac, "I can keep myself entertained until you return. So where are the bikes?"

Ezer leads Isaac to the far end of the workshop and past La Dauphine. Isaac is expecting to see a bike rack of mountain bikes and racing bikes or perhaps, knowing Ezer, some vintage or even antique bikes! Ezer points to two different sized contraptions staggered and angled to present distinctive side profiles.

The first thing that comes to Isaac's mind is an image of *a child's trike* quickly replaced with one of a *penny farthing*. Each bike has an exaggerated large front wheel and two side by side rear wheels. The front wheel has a fat black thick-treaded tyre and a red covered inner with a centrally positioned pedal. The rear wheels are much smaller than the front but with fatter black thick-treaded tyres, almost spherical.

There is no external chain or gear mechanism. Then Isaac clocks the *flying dolphin* bike frame, moulded in glass fibre and sprayed in a metallic gold sparkling paint. Each back wheel mounts to a *tail fluke* and can articulate together or independently where the flukes meet the body.

The main body sweeps up and over the front wheel. The front wheel forks are painted in satin matt black and enter underneath to join the handlebar arrangement. The *melon head* is circular in plan-view and rotates with the handlebars, sweeping left and right and protected with black handle grip ends. The *rostrum snout* is fixed and distinctive with the *dolphin's happy smile* housing a discrete wraparound strip of LED lights. The *dorsal fin* acts as the seat bracket with two individual seat pads mounted either side, all adjusted on the dolphin's back to accommodate different rider ergonomics. In each *blowhole* is a connector cable running back to the wall and into a square black box where two backlit displays show *full bars*.

Ezer is loving the surprise in Isaac's face and remains silent until the time is right, beginning,

"Our friend's electric!
The hub hides clever gearing
and *power assist!*

The tyres are made for
all terrains and the brakes are
controlled by the gears -

green button for *go...*
to *increase* gears. *Red* button
to decrease and stop!

You still pedal for
extra power and steer in
the familiar way!"

Ezer gives Isaac a demonstration before fetching two helmets and two pairs of gloves, handing one set to Isaac, adding,

"Take off your glasses.
These cool helmets have inbuilt
sensors and displays,

and can be set to
accommodate different
eyesight prescriptions!"

Isaac removes his spectacles and applies the helmet, clipping it securely beneath his chin. The helmet is bright yellow with a distinctive dark tinted inbuilt visor resembling *wasp eyes*, going up and over the front of his head to give an additional peripheral view, projected into the lower section of the visor. There are yellow lit orientation, speed and gravitational force displays on the inside visor. A small battery indicator confirms *full power*. A simple button on the helmet side automatically adjusts the integral lenses until everything is crystal clear. It's refreshing for Isaac not to wear spectacles or contact lenses...brilliant!

Ezer suggests a gentle introduction, opening the side door and escorting Isaac around to the enclosed courtyard. Isaac has never experienced *power assist* or riding such a bike. The handlebars are much wider and higher than normal. There is no crouching or race position. His back is almost vertical, and his legs are angled at forty-five degrees. Because his legs straddle the wheel and his feet connect to the pedals on the central hub, the front wheel movement is significantly and deliberately restricted. It feels awkward until Ezer further demonstrates and details,

"The rear wheels are your
stabilisers. You cannot
fall over. Promise!

Trust in your tail flukes.
Lean hard right to turn right. Lean
hard left to turn left!"

Isaac watches as Ezer swings left and right with little front steering - each tail fluke helping to pivot and steer, depending on how much force Ezer exerts on each seat pad to shift the centre of gravity. Every time Isaac tries, he improves. The bike's inbuilt sensors detect any obstacles and intervene to avoid any mishaps, blinking *warning signs* in the visor display and giving three sharp *beeps* in his left or right ear. Fifteen minutes pass.

"I think I'm ready now, Ezer," Isaac shouts across the courtyard. "Let's ride!"

"Press both *red* and *green*
buttons. This sets the *sheep mode*
where you follow me

and do everything I
do, automatically...
until you feel safe!"

Isaac and Ezer leave the courtyard. Ezer begins pedalling fast, pressing *green* and rattling through the gears. Isaac follows, watching his speedometer getting faster and faster!

12
Would you like to try my *Tricolour!?*

Leaving the confines of the courtyard, Ezer cycles up a narrow gravel path with the rear garden to his right and a field of grazing cows to his left. Ezer allows the local farmer to graze his animals in exchange for fresh produce and a free grass cutting service!

The gravel path ends as they enter the woods. The path turns into a mud track, showing signs of rainy day cycle rides - the top surface rutted and set like a cottage pie topping.

The going gets tougher and bumpier. Isaac is thankful for the superior padding on his split seat and observes what easy work the fat tyres make of the uneven terrain. The ruts soon disappear as the woods become denser - the rain-hogging trees making underfoot flatter and more even. Everywhere is covered in a blanket of dried leaves. Isaac gets a flash of déjà vu. If he didn't know he was in the woods next to Ezer's house, he would swear he was back in the school woods!

Isaac checks his speed in his visor. They're going twenty-five miles an hour...uphill! He has no idea where he's going or whether he could find his way back alone! Saying that, his visor pulses as it acknowledges a transmitting beacon connected to a birch trunk on his right, recording the journey and detailing their progress on a simple map Isaac can see when he looks to the top of his visor.

They reach the crest of the incline and take a sharp left, banking at speed as if the track has been specially contoured. There are a series of chicanes before the track turns into a wooden slatted decking overhanging a stream. There is no crash barrier, only a rope handrail. Ezer navigates them over this section with reassuring expertise and rejoins the mud track as they cross the stream and head right. Isaac can feel the gears in his front hub change down as they begin to climb again, changing up again and again as they gather speed.

They spook a red deer on their left which frightens Isaac just as much when it runs erratically alongside for a split second. The bikes are remarkably silent given their complexity, but that's the beauty of electric pedal power.

Isaac thinks about disengaging the *sheep mode* but thinks twice when Ezer takes on a bump in the track, and they take off...landing on their back wheels with a thud before the front wheel lands to help regain control. It's fantastic!

The track narrows and carves between two rocks before opening into a clearing. Sunlight shines down and temporarily blinds them until the visors compensate by further darkening the tint. Isaac can feel the heat on his arms helping to evaporate the sweat building up from his pedalling exertion. The centre of the clearing shows signs of a previous bonfire - the grass blackened and dead...the charcoal remnants are slowly decaying.

Ezer pulls them to a stop. He turns to Isaac and says,

"What do you think of
it so far? *Rubbish!* No, what
do you think so far?"

"These bikes are amazing, Ezer," replies Isaac, "and the woods are by far the best place to ride!"

"Would you like to see
Gravity Falls? We have to
climb higher. OK?"

enquires Ezer, vaguely gesturing with his right hand somewhere the other side of the clearing.

"Absolutely!" excites Isaac, "Definitely."

"Why don't you try to
ride unaided? Disengage
sheep mode. We'll go slow!"

suggests Ezer, watching Isaac's eyes widen as if he's seen a ghost.

"O..K...," says Isaac tentatively before responding with determination, "YES. I CAN DO THIS!"

Initially, Isaac wishes he could be back on the chequered courtyard - level and open, but the slower pace makes it so much easier. He now has time to think and plan his next move, gaining confidence with every ten-metre climb.

At one point, Isaac feels like he's on *La Grande Corniche*, snaking his way up a steady flow of hairpin bends - some naturally formed and others humanmade, only accessible by foot or bike.

Something catches Isaac's eye. Above him is a rail. It is reasonably discrete being made from polished stainless steel and reflecting its surroundings, but it's not something one expects to find floating in the woods. It follows a different path occasionally crossing over. Isaac spies the odd vertical support disguised as a tree with sprouting boughs and purposely rust coloured. Then it disappears, and Isaac doesn't see it again.

Ezer and Isaac arrive by a small lake encircled by woods and a lakeside path. On the far side is a wooden boathouse jettying several meters. They turn left and follow the path clockwise until they reach the boathouse and stop.

"Where's Gravity Falls?" asks Isaac as he removes his helmet and dismounts, putting on his spectacles once more.

"I don't want you to
see them...you must be at one
with Gravity Falls!"

replies Ezer with a sense of mischief and a menacing smile, as he opens the boathouse door and gestures for Isaac to follow, continuing,

"You must be hungry!
I am. Let's have lunch before
we do anymore!"

"But we're miles from home," exclaims Isaac, puzzled by Ezer's comments about Gravity Falls, "and I didn't think we brought anything with us."

Ezer says nothing. He claps three times. The lights turn on, and he walks over to a small bar area, opens a fridge and takes out a selection of ingredients. Isaac joins him at the bar, pulling himself onto one of the three bar stools, each coloured in red, yellow or green leather. With knife poised, Ezer looks at Isaac and asks,

"Would you like to try
my *Tricolour* - a ham, cheese
and spinach sandwich?

How hungry are you?
Can you eat a horse or do
I expect too much?"

"A *small* horse!" replies Isaac, watching Ezer fetch a fresh loaf and begin cutting lengthways, "I can maybe stretch to a pony!"

Ezer lays a slice of bread on a wooden board. Having rinsed the spinach, he meticulously covers the bread slice, taking care to overlap each leaf like a roof tiler laying tiles and repeats this until the layer is five millimetres thick. He takes a slab of apple smoked cheddar and using a special knife which has an adjustable measure, he cuts ten five-millimetre thick strips and places them on top of the spinach, working *left to right* and butting each strip so that every inch is covered. He seasons and then places the ham on the chopping board. Isaac has never seen such red ham.

"Gosh, Ezer!" gasps Isaac, "How did you get it to be so red?"

"It has been soaking
in tomato marinade
for thirty-three days!"

Ezer replies, cutting a small sample for Isaac to try.

"Oh, that's good!" declares Isaac, tasting the infusion of sun-dried Spanish tomatoes, paprika and balsamic vinegar, "Really good!"

Ezer uses the same special knife, carving four five-millimetre strips and laying them on top of the cheese. He tops with another slice of bread and carefully cuts the crusts off until he's left with a five-layered slab measuring ninety-nine millimetres wide and two hundred and ninety-seven millimetres long. He then cuts the slab into three long strips measuring thirty-three millimetres wide and offers one to Isaac.

Isaac lifts the sandwich with two hands, admiring the *Tricolour* red, yellow and green masterpiece, as he takes his first bite. Nothing is said. Ezer and Isaac consume their strips, indulging in a personal experience of simple food excellence. They agree to share the last strip and finish with a glass of ice cold water. Lunch doesn't get much better than this!

Ezer disappears into a small room opposite the bar and returns inconceivably quick, dressed in a red wetsuit again with a yellow side stripe and a flying dolphin on the back. He holds out a similar green wetsuit for Isaac, instructing,

"Please change into this
while I prepare *les dauphins*,
ready for our trip!"

Isaac takes the wetsuit and changes in the small room. When he returns, the boathouse has been transformed. Covers have been rolled back revealing two lake channels either side of a central walkway. The channels are lit by underwater lights turning the water a magical blue colour, and in each channel rests a golden dolphin!

"When you said *les dauphins*, I thought you were talking about vintage rowing boats!" exclaims Isaac, nervously, watching the dolphins bob up and down, half submerged, "To row over to Gravity Falls."

"Relax, Isaac! They're
watertight, pedal driven
and easy to steer!"

explains Ezer, opening the top hatch with integral dorsal fin, and sliding the pedal mechanism forwards to suit Isaac's height, continuing,

"Lie on your stomach,
grip the simple nose steer, and
pedal with your feet!"

Isaac climbs into the dolphin, lays on his stomach, places his feet on the pedals, grips the push-pull nose steer and looks straight ahead through the clear flush windscreen. As Ezer lowers the clear hatch, showing Isaac how to lock and unlock, Isaac shouts, "How much air time do I have?"

"The blowhole is a
special air *in and out* valve
- allows no water!"

shouts Ezer, giving Isaac the diver's sign for OK, adding,

"Just follow me and
all will unfold. Whatever
happens, keep smiling!"

Isaac fills with both trepidation and excitement. He watches Ezer leave his channel, and he begins pedalling. The pedal action is more back and forth than round and round, and the efficient gears transform little effort into big effect.

The sun glistens on the rippling water and glints on the gold metallic paint. There is no one around. No one to witness two *dolphins* swimming in a freshwater lake!

Isaac wonders what happens if he pushes both nose steering levers forwards. The nose dips and Isaac dives - water engulfing him as he submerges a few feet with only a dorsal fin visible above the surface. Isaac looks down to discover a small porthole. The lake water is clear, and he can see small minnows swimming beneath...and a trout...and a carp.

Ezer and Isaac edge towards the far left of the lake. Isaac is unsure, but he feels like he's accelerating without any more effort on his behalf. The lake is narrowing, converging to one point like Ezer's rear garden. Isaac doesn't need to pedal anymore. It's as if he's a rubber duck in a child's bath being drawn to the outlet after the plug is pulled.

Isaac keeps his eyes fixed on Ezer, some five metres ahead. Ezer then disappears from view!

Five seconds later and Isaac follows.

"EZER...FOOOOOL!" screams Isaac as he flies off Gravity Falls, one moment like a bird, the next gracefully diving headfirst thirty feet into a deep pool before being swished around in the fast-moving undercurrents and a tirade of bubbles. Isaac pulls his nose levers, and he begins his ascent, breaking through the surface as if to fly again, then bellyflopping horizontally, bobbing until he reaches a standstill some distance from the falls. He pedals over to Ezer, yelling, "That was fantastic, Ezer! I want to do it again!"

"So much better to
fly off Gravity Falls! We
can do it again!"

shouts Ezer, nodding at Isaac and leading him around to the left-hand side of Gravity Falls, where a special conveyor belt engages with the underside of each *dolphin* and escalators them back to the side of the lake to begin again.

Ezer and Isaac fly off Gravity Falls three more times before deciding to make their way back to the boathouse.

It is the most exhilarating thing that Isaac has ever done, and he can't wait to do it again. He likens it to eating Ezer's Newton apple flavoured fudge for breakfast, lunch and dinner...not forgetting afternoon tea!

13

The Angry Wasp!

Ezer helps Isaac out of his dolphin and suggests that Isaac changes first while he batons down the boathouse hatches.

"I wish I could take a warm shower," comments Isaac, standing on the central walkway, and shivering like a fish out of water, "the lake's pretty cold...even with a wetsuit!"

"Once stripped, stand on the
golden circle, and clap thrice
for the *shower cloak!*"

recommends Ezer without looking at Isaac, securing each dolphin with a rigid metal arm to its blowhole.

Puzzled, Isaac ventures into the small room. Sure enough, he finds the golden circle in the middle of the floor. Undressed, he stands as instructed and claps thrice! Expecting a stream of water to shower down from the ceiling, he is startled when the silver ring, lining the golden circle begins to move upwards. His instinct is to jump off, but he remains to survey the cylindrical frosted glass *shower cloak* move gradually up and surround his body.

Nine inches above the ground, a downward conical water jet bursts from the silver ring inner circumference, tickling his feet like fine pins and needles, preparing and massaging the skin as it goes. Isaac feels like a car in a carwash as the conical jet moves slowly but surely up his body! He spies three different indicator lights in the ceiling. The first light glows *yellow*. As the water caresses the crown of his head, it automatically detects his height, changing direction and exchanging the jet of water for a fine spray of scented soap. When the spray passes his midriff,

Isaac rubs his hair and then his body, releasing the pleasant aroma of sweet apple, invigorating and cleansing his body with sensitivity and the perfect pH balance. Isaac is relieved when the shower cloak reaches his feet to begin again - when the second light glows *green*, a vigorous water jet, set to precisely fifty-five degrees Celsius, replaces the soap spray...and not, as he feared for a second, a body scrubbing set of chammy leather flannels!

The shower cloak moves up and down his body at the ideal speed, rinsing the soap suds as it goes. Isaac watches the waste water run into the floor around the golden circle - the shower cloak wall ensuring none escapes contaminating the surrounding room. The final light glows *red*. Water is substituted by an equally intense jet of hot air, again at fifty-five degrees Celsius, set to evaporate the remaining droplets on his wet body. Reaching his head, it detects the contours of his face and narrows the stream of hot air to focus on his hair. The temperature increases to sixty-five degrees Celsius, and the movement slows. As the shower cloak begins its final descent, a fine moisturising spray accompanies the hot air jet, *wrapping* Isaac in his own apple scented cloak.

The shower cloak becomes the floor once more, drying the golden circle on its way through, and all evidence of any shower activity. The *start to finish* cycle is exactly three minutes!

Isaac hangs his wetsuit on a hanger, puts on his green lycra suit, and exits the small room. Ezer is already standing in his red lycra suit, and handing Isaac a small golden droplet, saying with a cheesy grin,

"Chocolate Surprise!
Thought you'd like a sugar-hit
before we head home!"

Isaac puts on his helmet again, and notices the diminished battery level in his visor, warning, "We don't have much power left, Ezer!"

"Don't worry, Isaac!
The return is much quicker,
and it's all downhill!"

reassures Ezer, turning his bike to face downhill, adding,

"There is a *special
track*, or a gentle path home.
Which one would you like?"

Isaac ponders for a moment before replying, "The special track! As long as I can go first!"

Ezer says nothing, admiring Isaac's courage. He leads him to the start line, counting him down with a changing finger wave of three, two, one, go!

As Isaac works his way through the gears, aided by gravity and power assist, his helmet speakers start playing the theme tune to *The Good, The Bad and The Ugly!* The cycle track winds and weaves, wobbles and wreaks havoc to the changing tempo and tune of this iconic score, occasionally inducing Isaac to scream, "Aa...aa...aargh!" as he takes the corner too fast or finds himself taking off, and wondering whether the land will ever again be his friend! His cycling is all three - mostly *good*, sometimes *bad* and occasionally, frighteningly *ugly!* The fanfare of trumpets brings him home, crossing the finish line in a flurry of flying leaves, stirred into action by his side angle braking.

Ezer joins him, stopping to applaud and give Isaac a respectful bow before they fall into fits of raucous laughter.

As the frivolities subside, Isaac spies the overhead rail again, this time snaking its way closer to the ground.

"What's that?" Isaac asks Ezer, pointing to the rail.

"I wondered when you'd
ask! It's a roller coaster
called *The Angry Wasp!*"

responds Ezer, shaking his head and tutting before checking his watch, adding,

"Think the bikes are fun!
Just wait till you've felt the sting
of *The Angry Wasp!*"

Isaac follows Ezer. His interest is ignited with sparks of intrigue and fascination...just when he thought the day couldn't get any better!

They come to an enormous grey pointed egglike pod. It looks like molten lava or swirling marble, but as they get closer, Isaac is taken aback by its paper-like quality. He then spots the rail passing through the structure via two central side holes.

Ezer claps three times, saying mischievously,

"Welcome to the wasp's
nest. Home to *The Angry Wasp.*
Let the ride begin!"

A circular door automatically opens, lowering like a drawbridge to create an enticing ramp, drawing Isaac and Ezer through to the illuminated interior, now pulsating with a yellow glow. Ezer and Isaac wheel in their bikes and remove their helmets.

Isaac discovers *The Angry Wasp* for the first time. A nine-foot-long monster! Its terrifying triangular head is five feet wide with great big black eyes, pronounced mandibles, and dramatic yellow and black markings. Behind the head is a black thorax mid body, joining at the waist to the distinctive yellow and black striped abdomen...swaging to an endpoint and a needle-sharp *sting*. There are two seats in the thorax, and a central seat just behind at the beginning of the abdomen, all upholstered in black leather with yellow piping, and all housing rigid over-the-shoulder safety harnesses. There are polished chrome handrails. Either side of the thorax sprouts transparent wings, doubling as access platforms and edged in black rubber. Three pairs of segmented yellow legs dangle beneath - pointing frontwards, sideways and backwards. The Angry Wasp has a poised rake to add to the theatre, and two black antennae provide the finishing touches.

Ezer helps Isaac onto the wing and into the front cockpit, following closely behind. As he pushes a red button on the front dashboard to lower and lock all three harnesses into position, Ezer side glances Isaac, pushes the green start button and says,

"Hold on to the rail!
It's *gonna* be three minutes
like you've never had!"

The Angry Wasp moves off to the right and begins its ascent, storing potential energy to convert into kinetic energy as it goes!

Isaac can feel the undercarriage being pulled along by some mechanical force within the rail. The rail attempts to take the shortest route but often steers right then left to avoid trees and bushes, adding to its complexity. What is sure, is that the higher The Angry Wasp goes, the more stored energy it accrues.

The Angry Wasp creeps uphill posing no threat to the wildlife, who seem puzzled by its existence, but innately suspicious of its colouring and markings. Squirrels look twice before darting up the nearest tree. A fallow deer alarm calls its foal to run scared in the opposite direction.

Isaac takes this opportunity to admire the woods and to catch brief glimpses of rolling countryside, deep-breathing in the natural aromas of horse chestnut and English oak as they calmly meander their way - the vertical rail supports growing in stature and realigning the sight line.

Like a charged bow, The Angry Wasp reaches the top and unleashes itself with a ferocious roar. A roar made by Ezer and Isaac, screaming, "Aaarrrggghhh!!!" as they descend into complete mayhem, twisting and turning, spiralling and looping, flipping and swaying...around and through treetops... frolicking with birds who view them with shrills of concern. When the loops get smaller, they accelerate, when they straighten out the momentum carries them on, keeping them glued to their seats - G-force and inertia playing tricks with their sense of direction, sometimes adding weightlessness into the mix, or forcing them so far into their seats that they can feel the springs resisting and fighting back. It is one very Angry Wasp!

They skirt this morning's stream and get a pair of short sightings of Gravity Falls!

Isaac spies the special bike track as they fly upside down, hanging on by the seat of their pants. Then it ends. The Angry Wasp pulls up like a reined in horse. Its sting - lost, perhaps somewhere in the woods or as one final shot on target to bring Ezer and Isaac *home* to nest.

"That was incredible!" shouts Isaac, pulling out his heart from inside his stomach, and vehemently shaking his head left and right. "AGAIN, EZER, AGAIN!"

Ezer predicts such a response, already pressing the green button!

"What's the yellow button for, Ezer?" asks Isaac, collecting himself as they begin *the calm before the storm* again.

"The Angry Wasp has sound effects. I forgot! Let's turn up the volume!"

replies Ezer, pressing the yellow button and smiling.

Ezer and Isaac ride The Angry Wasp twice more, imagining themselves in a *Huey* helicopter - under enemy attack, and manoeuvring around the woods to complete a covert mission.

It's supper time.

Ezer and Isaac leave The Angry Wasp for another day and return their bikes to the workshop. They agree to meet in the rear garden in fifteen minutes.

Changed back into the clothes he first wore - what feels like a hundred hours earlier that day! Isaac bounds through to the rear garden to find Ezer dressed as Chef Strangeman, cooking tonight's meal on the BBQ and throwing a ball to Copernicus.

"Sit yourself down. Three more minutes and my *five-star burgers* are ready!"

announces Ezer, preparing the buns and relish.

Isaac expects nothing else. The five-pointed star burgers are cooked to perfection with just the right amount of seasoning, the tastiest of green apple relish, the most succulent of melting

Manchego cheese, and all housed in a mouth-watering five-pointed star brioche bun. And the chips aren't bad either!

After three games of chess, Ezer...the victor again, asks Isaac if he would like to play billiards.

"Sure," replies Isaac, "I've played a few times at school."

Ezer takes the plates and cooking items inside. He returns, again inconceivably quickly, dressed in a crisp white shirt with a golden bow tie, red trousers and a matching waistcoat sporting a green silk back. His shoes are polished black and covered in white spats. Two metal armbands pull his sleeves taut. His ginger red hair is greased back and placed in a ponytail. Isaac can't work out how, but Ezer also has a pencil moustache...genuine and precisely defined!

Copernicus runs over, unsure of Ezer's identity. He repeatedly smells Ezer before being convinced and returns to the lawn.

"Wow, Ezer!" remarks Isaac, feeling underdressed and put at a significant disadvantage, "It looks like you mean business!"

Ezer smiles, ignoring his comment, and says proudly,

"I have invented
Black Hole Billiards, also
called *SNOOKANOVA!*
Come play on my new
table - using three balls, five
stars and one black hole!"

14
The big bang!

Ezer opens the door to the house located opposite the garden dining area and directly below his room. He ushers in Isaac, clapping three times to breathe life into a sleeping room.

They walk down a short dark passage, through a secondary door and into a white pentagonal room. Once in, the secondary door closes to encapsulate the room fully. This door is round-arched and all black. It has a black velvet bench seat and a padded black velvet recess, buttoned and crimped like an antique Chesterfield sofa. Each pentagon side has a similar black recessed seating area, possibly doubling as doors, but Isaac is unsure.

Isaac gazes at the midnight blue ceiling covered in tiny LED lights, sparkling like distant stars in the night sky. In the centre of the ceiling is a brushed stainless steel pentagonal light fitting, shining *shadow-less* light onto the table below.

And there it is. The SNOOKANOVA table - a deep blue felt covered pentagon with a golden *star* pocket in each corner and a single bigger *black hole* pocket, dead centre. There is a fine-line five-pointed gold star printed on the fabric with each outer apex pointing to a corner pocket. The table edge is brushed stainless steel fixed to a straight wall white marble plinth. Isaac estimates the distance between pockets to be five feet and each room wall to be thirteen feet, giving the perfect shot-making distance in-between.

Ezer selects two cues from the five-cue rack and hands a polished white cue to Isaac together with a cube of yellow chalk. The cue is a traditionally tapered round cue with a green tip. The butt end is pentagonal, created by five arced cuts running out along the cue. The butt end has an inlaid polished green star, sitting like a jewel in a crown. Ezer's cue is identical, but his butt star is red.

Ezer collects three balls from the centre black hole and places them on the central star. One ball is red, another is yellow, and the last one is green. Ezer turns to Isaac to explain the rules,

"The game is multi-directional. No pocket, ball hierarchy.

It's time-based - five minutes or one day. Agree the time - most points wins!

Up to five players. No bridges or extensions ...climbing or cheating!

Balls - any order, any star point, in or out... at *start*, after pot!

You can't pot a ball directly - only *in* and *off* another ball!

Cannon - when cue ball hits both balls or cue ball hits one...hits another!

Cannon or pot - *one point*. Cannon and pot - *three points*. Cannon...two pots - *five!*

Cannon...three pots - *ten*. No point - next player. Ball in *The Black Hole* - you lose!"

"Run that by me again, Ezer!" says Isaac, watching Ezer's face turn from one of intense focus to losing the will to live! Adding, "Only joking! Perhaps a practice game to start?"

They toss a coin. Ezer wins.

Ezer goes to one of the black recesses and dials *ten minutes* into the scoreboard, appearing big and bold in white backlit numbers. An identical scoreboard illuminates in each recess. The scoreboards are flush mounted circular black screens with different coloured backlit numerical displays for each player. He turns off three to leave two - the red and green displays, and presses *start*. The clock starts ticking down.

Ezer hits the yellow ball and cannons into the green. One point. He hits the green to go in off the red ball. Another point. He places the green ball on an outer star apex close to the yellow ball. He uses the yellow ball to hit the green ball and try for a cannon, but misses! It's Isaac's turn.

Isaac hits the red ball into a star pocket off the yellow ball. The yellow ball cannons into the green. Three points.

"Beginner's luck!" exclaims Isaac, retrieving the red ball and choosing his preferred apex. His next shot sees the green cannon into the red and then the yellow. One point. The following shot is no points. Ezer dials in four points, dwarfing his two points!

Ezer lines up the green ball to cannon into the yellow and then the red. It hits the yellow, but his contact is too thin, and the green ball takes a different angle off the cushion, hitting another cushion and then rolling as if in slow-motion, into *the black hole!*

"You lose, Ezer!" declares Isaac, disguising a laugh, "You disappeared into *The Back Hole!*"

"I have invented
the game, but I never said
I was very good!"

admits Ezer, picking the green ball out of the black hole and handing it to Isaac.

Isaac resets the table to his liking while Ezer resets the timer, this time setting it to thirty minutes. Isaac and Ezer play three games before Isaac finds himself falling asleep in one of the recesses just as Ezer finds his form and gets on a roll!

"I can't keep my eyes open, Ezer," says Isaac, stifling a yawn, "do you mind if we pause and carry on tomorrow? *One all* with this game *a decider* requires full concentration, and my heads full of bike rides and angry wasps!"

"No problem, Isaac.
Don't forget - I'm off in the
morn' 'till eleven!"
replies Ezer, replacing the cues in the rack and leading Ezer through another door into the front hall.

"Night, Ezer. Thank you for a wonderful day. I can't tell you how much I've enjoyed it!" says Isaac, giving Ezer a hug and turning to go upstairs, "Have a great morning. I look forward to seeing you when you return."

"I will prepare food
and leave it out for you. Help
yourself. Sweet dreams. Night!"
informs Ezer, heading for the kitchen, Copernicus in tow.

Isaac opens his bedroom door and claps three times. Walking the short distance upstairs has awoken him with just enough energy to climb the spiral staircase to view the stars once more. He promises himself fifteen minutes before brushing his teeth and climbing into bed. No sooner does his head hit the pillow than he falls into the land of Nod.

Isaac forgets to close his shutters or curtains again and wakes to a stream of light hitting his face and warming him like a stove fried egg. He's hungry - it must be breakfast time. Isaac tries to read his watch before remembering he hasn't put on his spectacles. He searches the bedside table, patting around like a toddler discovering a piano!

"Nine o'clock!" reads Isaac as his eyes adjust under the guidance of his faithful glasses, "I wonder if Ezer's left yet?"

He jumps out of bed to hear La Dauphine backfire. Running over to the orchard window, he catches sight of Ezer as a flicker of yellow paint through the bushes by the driveway to the left of the orchard. Ezer disappears towards the front gate.

Isaac sits on the window seat and pulls his legs up to enjoy the view. Legs crossed, he puts his hands behind his head and smiles to himself as he remembers yesterday's events. Two turtle doves distract him as they perch on the top of a plum tree, cooing as if swapping stories and meeting for a *catch-up!*

A wasp breaks his concentration, tapping at the window as if to say hello before heading off in a completely random direction. Isaac wonders how angry the wasp is, closing his eyes to ride the roller coaster once more.

His eyes open when he begins to laugh at Ezer's misfortune of falling into the black hole in SNOOKANOVA!

Then something glints on the far orchard wall and catches Isaac's eye. He removes his spectacles to give them a thorough clean, finding them filthy and clouding his view. Replacing them, he looks again to see another glint. There are two ladder ends sticking over the top of the wall like a *Punch and Judy* puppet show. Isaac isn't sure whether the ladder is always there, and the sun's angle is highlighting it, or whether it is a new addition.

Just as Isaac begins to look away, he sees another ladder being hoisted and pushed over to lean against the inside wall. Then a figure, bold as brass and cast in shadow, climbs up and over, followed by another. The trespassers collect themselves, tip the ladder horizontally and carry it to the centre of the orchard without any apparent fear or risk of being caught. Isaac is sure that they're kids - they're far too small to be adults.

"They must have waited until Ezer left," Isaac thinks to himself, rationalising further, "and they don't know that I remained. Perhaps they don't even know that I'm here!"

It is then that Isaac sees the ladder being elevated against Newton's tree, making him gasp and cry out, "They're scrumping Newton's apples. I must stop them!"

Isaac doesn't think to knock on the window. He dresses quickly in yesterday's gear, thrown uncharacteristically on the floor the night before, and rushes downstairs. Copernicus is waiting at the foot of the stairs, oblivious to the orchard ongoings.

"Great guard dog, you are!" exclaims Isaac, patting him on the head. He opens the front door, and they head for the orchard. One of Isaac's laces isn't tied properly. It nearly sends him flying when Copernicus stands on it as if he's trying to trip him up!

Isaac is about to open the grey gate to the orchard when he stops to consider his well-being, agonising, "What if they're bigger than me and beat me up! What if they've got a weapon!"

He then thinks of Ezer's apple flavoured fudge! It consumes him with rage, and like an angry wasp, he throws the gate open and rushes in, shouting, "GET OFF THOSE APPLES, YOU THIEVES!"

Copernicus follows but runs the other way when he spies a squirrel scuttling along the orchard floor.

The apple scrumpers jump into action, grabbing their half-full bag and ladder, and run towards the end orchard wall. Isaac isn't sure what he's going to do when he catches up with them. All he knows is that he must retrieve Newton's apples!

He runs past a plum tree and into the apple column. The apple scrumpers are nearing the rear wall. Isaac remembers the Sports Day relay race, imagining the thieves as the white tape finish line.

As he approaches Newton's tree, the front of his right shoe lodges in a raised root. He trips, rolling head first into Newton's tree! It sparks a chain reaction, the chances of which the finest mathematicians couldn't forecast. As he falls to the floor, *the big bang* simultaneously dislodges a red apple, a golden apple and a green apple, coincidentally hanging at the same height above the ground.

Each with a mass of one hundred and two grams, the apples fall with a one Newton force at nine point eight metres per second every second, hitting Isaac on the back of his head at the *exact same* time, dishing out a three-Newton blow to the head!

It knocks him out cold. He lays on the orchard floor...transported to a land of sweet dreams.

The apple scrumpers make a speedy exit with their spoils in hand!

15
An anti-gravity device!

"GOT YOU!" exclaims Isaac, grabbing the right ankle of the second apple scrumper scrambling up the inside ladder, "No one's stealing apples on my watch!"

The other apple scrumper is standing on the outside ladder playing tug-of-war with Isaac to pull his *partner in crime* to freedom.

"Get off me!" shrills the voice of a young girl, trying to shake free from Isaac's tightening hold, "Who do you think you are - the apple police!?"

"They are not your apples to take!" replies Isaac, now gripping her ankle with two hands and holding to his chest, "Give them back!"

"Have your stupid apples!" shouts the voice of a young boy - the other apple scrumper, "Just let her go!"

A small canvas bag flies over the wall and lands on the floor, spilling three apples - one red, one yellow and one green. Isaac is flabbergasted that the scrumpers have surrendered Newton's apples so easily. The young girl wriggles free at the expense of her right shoe. Isaac is left holding a red boot! It's no *glass slipper*, and she's no *Cinderella* - the boot is worn out and a bit whiffy!

"All that fuss over three apples!" the apple scrumpers shout as they scurry down the outside ladder and escape into the meadow ...empty *red-handed*!

Isaac picks up the three apples and puts them into the small canvas bag, along with the girl's red boot. Aware of their magnificent taste, Isaac is tempted to try an apple. He knows he should seek Ezer's permission, but he can blame the apple scrumpers if he's ever cross-examined!

Isaac picks out the red apple and takes a huge bite. It's the most delicious concentration of intense flavour Isaac has ever tasted - as if all of nature's red fruits have been crammed together and fused to create a rich harmony of sweetness. There is a fiery aftertaste as he swallows to make room for the next bite. He sits down by Newton's tree to enjoy this special moment and leans against the trunk.

As Isaac finishes the red apple, he is compelled to experience the others and takes a bite from the golden apple. Its intense flavour is on a par, but instead of red fruits, there is a fusing of rich *gloopy* honey and delicate golden nectar balanced with hints of lemon and lime citrus, and a wisp of orange to offset any bitterness. Isaac thinks it might be how the sun tastes...!

The green apple is different again, combining the flavours of gooseberry, rhubarb and grape and fizzing with a scintillating sparkle to mix its intense flavour with the airy scent of woods and flowering meadows. There is an earthy undertone, verging on savoury, but it is indescribably subtle and in no way undermining when comparing with the others.

While Isaac contemplates which apple he likes best, he makes swirling patterns in the dust with his right foot. Something gold coloured catches his eye. He sweeps the floor with his foot to uncover what looks like a metal badge. Now kneeling, Isaac uses his hands, and like an archaeologist delicately uncovering an ancient artefact, Isaac defines a triangular outline of what is looking more and more like a wooden box with an ornate brass badge and engraved initials, faded over time.

Isaac spits on the badge and rubs it with the inside of his denim jacket cuff. He discerns the initials, capital *N* and capital *I*, engraved in a lavish serif font, but as he moves his head to read them the other way, he sees they could equally read as *I* and *N*. *I* and *N*...*Isaac* and *Newton*. It's a box belonging to Isaac Newton!

Isaac can't contain his excitement. He runs to the workshop to fetch a tool - any tool to help excavate the box...Isaac Newton's box...now Isaac Newman's box!

It's not the best tool, and Isaac hopes that Ezer won't scold him for using one of his special super sharp chisels! He scrapes the hard-dry ground as if building a moat around a medieval castle. It takes time, and his sweat begins to drip onto the lid like early signs of rain. Isaac digs down four inches before the box begins to move. He rocks the box until it breaks free, tilting it to insert his right-hand underneath.

Isaac lifts the equilateral triangular box and places it on his knee, studying the details and wondering how it opens. The box could quite easily be one of Ezer's sandwiches if the top and bottom English oak wooden elements are the *bread*, and the central brass strip is the *cheese filling!*

Each side is about a foot long making the box similar in size to a snooker rack or a box to contain a full set of snooker balls. Isaac measures it later to be three hundred and three millimetres which is ironic given that metric didn't exist in Newton's era!

With the I.N. initials facing him, Isaac sees a full-length brass hinge along the top side, but there is no obvious catch or lock. Thankfully there appears to be no key escutcheon and therefore no lost key!

It's puzzling. How do you open a box that has no key or apparent latch? Has it seized or fused over time?

Isaac moves his fingers along the hinge as if it contains a secret braille message. The hinge stops three-quarters of an inch from each end. The metal feels slightly indented, indicative of its age. Isaac presses each shallow punt with his index fingers. They disappear into the box pushing a box-sized triangular brass wedge forwards to clear and disengage an internal lock, cleverly providing a lid-lifting handle at the same time! Ingenious!

Isaac lays the box on the ground and lifts the lid slowly. He hopes it doesn't contain some deadly disease or a poisonous snake - a trap to protect the contents within. Isaac shakes his head - sometimes his imagination runs wild!

The lid moves through one hundred and eighty degrees, resting beautifully against the lower half to create a brass rhombus platter with all sides equal in length and identical opposing angles. It is pristine and highly polished - despite its age. The open lid has three circular scoops uniformly set into the brass, and each scoop has a further central indent. The lower half also has three circular scoops uniformly set into the brass, except this time there are three brightly coloured translucent glass apples suspended in each scoop. There is a red apple at the front, a yellow apple top left, and a green apple top right, all with polished silver pointed stems protruding from an inner core. Isaac sees that the inner core is gold - a five-pointed star when viewed from above, and heart-shaped when viewed from the side. The apples look good enough to eat!

Isaac also notices a small number engraved by each apple. Red has *one* - yellow has *two*...green has *three*.

He picks up *red apple number one* and cups it in both hands as if tentatively holding a bird with a damaged wing. The apple weighs one hundred and two grams. Inside its respective scoop is a small point onto which it was suspended.

Isaac turns the apple upside down to get a better view, but his hands begin to float with an instant feeling of weightlessness! He immediately turns the apple upright which lowers his hands, making him shriek, "OMG, these apples are magic!"

Isaac stands up and moves to a clear spot between the trees. He turns the apple upside down as if setting an egg timer, and sure enough, it lifts upwards, raising his arms then taking him into the air and accelerating at nine point eight metres per second every second! Within a split second, Isaac is floating above the trees and climbing higher and higher!

He turns the apple upright only to fall to earth equally fast. Just before he slams into the ground, with the likely result of breaking his legs, he turns the apple upside down which has the effect of bringing him to a stop to rise again. He quickly rotates the apple upright once more to reach the ground as if casually stepping off a staircase bottom step.

"The red apple's *an anti-gravity device!*" declares Isaac, carefully replacing it in the box and glancing around to ensure no one is witnessing this amazing event, exclaiming, "It's a flying device!"

Isaac picks up the *yellow number two apple* and moves to the same clear spot between the trees. The yellow apple is identical in all aspects except for its translucent golden colour. Preparing to elevate, Isaac turns the apple away from him. Instead of moving upwards, it speeds away from him, accelerating at nine point eight metres per second every second. This figure might not break any land speed records, but when you're holding it in your hands it feels as fast as a moving bullet!

Isaac pulls it upright again, expecting the apple to return to its original spot. It remains motionless - his hands are outstretched. He turns the apple towards him, and sure enough, it travels backwards equally fast and surprises Isaac with a thump to his chest. In shock, Isaac drops the apple and watches it roll away - accelerating then changing direction when it collides with a tree trunk. Isaac chases after it as if he's comedically chasing a plastic bag in the wind. Just when he thinks the apple is lost in a state of perpetual motion, he dives on it like a goalkeeper making a winning save, grabbing the apple in both hands and pointing the silver stem to the sky.

"The yellow apple's *an accelerator device!*" declares Isaac, getting to his feet and replacing it in the box after a quick polish against his top, concluding, "A backwards and forwards device!"

After near catastrophe with the yellow apple, Isaac is cautious to discover the remaining apple's unique feature. He picks up the *green apple number three* and again moves to the clear spot between the trees. This time he's anticipating the unexpected.

He turns the apple. As it turns a quarter-turn, it moves in the opposite direction. He turns it back upright, and it stops. He turns it a quarter-turn the other way, and it moves in the opposite

117

direction. Isaac turns it upright, and again it stops. "The green apple's *a direction device!*" he declares, confirming his assumption by holding out the apple in his right hand, quarter turning it to the right to watch his arm move to the left, then turning it to the left and watching his arm move right, exclaiming, "A *side to side* device!"

Isaac is reminded of Newton's Laws of Motion and Gravity. He takes out Ezer's folded note from his jacket pocket and rereads the simplistic explanations, applying the laws to the three apples. After considered rationalisation, Isaac checks the coast is clear and recites his conclusions aloud - he finds that it makes more sense to hear it relayed back even when it's him who's saying it!

"Newton's First Law is *red apple number one* where the apple will *move* when it is acted on by a Force - in this case, an *anti-gravity* force! Newton's Second Law *is yellow apple number two* where the acceleration of the one Newton apple is equal to its one Newton Force divided by its one hundred and two-gram Mass - making its acceleration nine point eight metres per second every second which remains constant regardless of any increase in mass and providing there are no other interfering forces! And Newton's Third Law is *green apple number three* where the action of turning the apple to the right has an equal and opposite reaction - moving the apple to the left and vice versa!"

Isaac is fired up. The respective apple numbers correlate with Newton's Laws. Now he wants to get all three apples working together. He closes the lid, pushes the triangular wedge back into position, places the box under his arm and heads for the workshop. The apples are held in suspended animation by Newton's clever core-holding method.

16
A rabbit called *Stew!*

Isaac is happy to skip breakfast - content with consuming three Newton apples! He enters the workshop door and places Newton's box on a clear bench area next to the golf cart seats. He decides not to open the box until he has a plan.

Isaac identifies one basic problem - there are three apples, and he only has two hands!

While he ponders his quandary, there are three taps on the workshop window. The male scrumper stands like a ghostly apparition - his green *hoody* pulled over his head and casting his face in deep shadow as if it doesn't exist!

Isaac lets out a yelp, holding his heart and shouting, "You frightened the life out of me!" before glancing at the small inner workshop door - ajar. He's overcome with a sense of vulnerability, nervously adding, "What do you want? I...'ve called the police!"

Isaac hasn't called the police, but the scrumpers don't know that!

"We want our shoe back!" shouts the scrumper, lifting his head slightly to throw light on his nose - a reassuring human sign, continuing, "You've got no use for it. Just give it back, and we'll leave you in peace."

He's right - Isaac has no use for the girl's boot, and it's an easy way to resolve this awkward encounter. Isaac grabs the canvas bag and exits the workshop. As he enters the courtyard and stands on a light-coloured paving slab, he sees the previously hidden female scrumper standing in front of him on a dark-coloured slab. She makes a move towards him, hobbling on one boot, revealing a bright yellow sock, covered in dust. She grimaces as she steps on a small stone. Wearing a yellow *hoody*, it places her face is in darkness, but two long red plaits secured with golden ties, hang down her front like two rope pulls. Both scrumpers are wearing denim jeans, identically ripped at the knee and showing same sized turn-ups.

Outnumbered, Isaac glances at each scrumper, assessing their similar heights - marginally taller than him. The young girl outstretches her hand to take the canvas bag while the young boy edges closer to Isaac's left, moving from a dark to a light slab. Like a knight under pincer attack from two pawns, Isaac decides his best form of defence is *attack!*

"Not so fast!" cries Isaac, placing the canvas bag behind his back, "I think you need to apologise first!"

Ten, twenty, thirty seconds pass. Finally, the young girl, now standing with her bootless right foot on her booted left foot, whispers, "I'm sorry!"

"I can't hear you!" replies Isaac, pushing his luck, "Louder! And I want to hear both of you...without your *hoodies!*"

The apple scrumpers swap telepathic glances, recognising that they don't have a leg to stand on - they did, after all, attempt to steal apples! The young boy replies, "We'll only say sorry if you call off the police!"

"Absolutely!" agrees Isaac with a sense of control.

One by one, the scrumpers unveil themselves, pushing their hoodies back with a tentative right-hand sweep. Isaac double-takes. They're not identical twins being *boy* and *girl* but exchange the boy's short ginger red hair to the girl's face, and the girl's long ginger red hair to the boy's face and anyone would struggle to tell them apart. They both have bright blue eyes with dark eyelashes, freckled cheeks and spectacles.

"You're twins!" exclaims Isaac, growing a smile, "And you're both wearing the same spectacles as mine!"

"I think you're wearing the same spectacles as ours!" replies the young boy, puffing out his chest as a primal gesture of bravado.

"Mine are far-sighted - with astigmatism in my left eye!" informs Isaac, unsure as to why he would engage them on such a topic but swayed by coincidence.

"Mine too!" adds the young girl, nodding and twitching her mouth, trying to suppress a habitual smile, adding to the annoyance of the young boy, "And my brother's the same, but astigmatism in his right eye!"

"Yeah, yeah!" adds the young boy, keen to keep his distance and disengage as quickly as possible. "So, we're sorry. There, we've said it. Now can we have her boot!"

Isaac hands the boot back to the young girl. She wrestles it from the canvas bag and pulls it on, stamping it on the floor three times to push in her foot to the end.

"I didn't call the police!" blurts Isaac, astonished by his needless honesty but sensing broken down barriers, adding, "I just said that earlier, in case you were going to beat me up!"

The young boy and girl laugh, but Isaac hasn't said anything funny.

"We're pacifists!" responds the young girl, managing to control her laughter.

"We love nature and animals," adds the young boy, "and believe in *love and peace* to all."

"We wouldn't hurt a fly!" says the young girl, ushering away an annoying bluebottle with a gentle wave, "See?"

"But the *hoodies*," says Isaac, pointing to each in turn. "They're menacing and make you look like a pair of hoodlums!"

"What would you wear if you went apple scrumping?" defends the young girl, unzipping her hoody by six inches.

"I suppose I'd cover my face in some way to make me difficult to identify!" admits Isaac, seeing their sense.

"We thought the old geezer lived alone!" remarks the young boy. "When did you arrive?"

"The day before yesterday," replies Isaac, stopping to think for a second, given how much he's done in such a short time, "My Uncle Ezer - the *old geezer* as you so delicately describe him, picked me up at the *end of term.*"

"Where do you go to school?" enquires the young girl, staring Isaac up and down like the fashion police!

"Down south!" replies Isaac. "What about you?"

"Grantham!" replies the young boy, looking at his sister and nodding.

"We get the bus every morning from the local village," details the young girl, "and then a lift back with our Mum...she's a teacher, but at another school that starts earlier!"

"Where do you live?" asks Isaac, more relaxed with every second and happy to have a conversation with someone who doesn't always speak in haiku!

"The other side of the cow field...just through the trees," replies the young boy, pointing in the general direction, "in a small cottage. Me, my Mum and my sister."

"And our pet rabbit - *Stew!*" adds the young girl, waiting for the penny to drop.

"You called your rabbit, Stew!?" laughs Isaac, enjoying the irony. "Brilliant! That's like calling a pet chicken, *Fajitas!*"

"Or calling a pet pig, *Bacon!*" adds the young boy, watching his sister and Isaac give puzzled looks.

"Not quite, Pip!" exclaims the young girl, shaking her head at Isaac and shrugging her shoulders.

"Pip!" says Isaac, holding out his hand, "I'm Isaac! It's a pleasure to meet you, even under these strange circumstances."

"Good to meet you, too, Isaac," replies Pip, shaking his hand and turning to his sister, "and this is my sister, Russet!"

"Russet!" repeats Isaac, shaking her hand, "What an unusual and beautiful name!"

Isaac and Russet blush. Why didn't Isaac comment on Pip's name? Darwin's got a lot to answer!

"Our Mum's got a sense of humour," injects Pip. "She says we're *the apple of her eye,* and with a surname like *Bramley*, how could we be anything else, but *Pippin and Russet Bramley!*"

"What does your Dad think of it?" asks Isaac, too late - remembering Pip's omission when describing his home.

"We don't know our Dad," replies Russet, "and our Mum never talks about him!"

"Apple scrumpers called *Pippin and Russet Bramley!*" outlines Isaac, "You couldn't make it up! What's your Mum's name?"

"Theresa!" replies Russet, embellishing, *"Trezer - Tree's a Bramley!* Can you believe it!"

Isaac tells Pip and Russet about his parents and spending the whole summer with his uncle. They discuss Ezer's idiosyncrasies and eccentricities and how this makes Pip and Russet cautious and scared of Ezer. Isaac reassures them that Ezer is *one in a million* and misunderstood - the coolest person, he's ever met!

"But why the apples?" enquires Isaac, "How did you know they ripen earlier than other apples?"

"Our Mum told us about them!" says Russet, "She says *they taste out of this world!*"

"How good are you at keeping secrets?" asks Isaac, identifying Pip and Russet as the extra hands he so urgently needs.

"Mum's the word!" replies Pip, fake zipping his mouth.

"Yeah! On *Rabbit Stew's* life!" declares Russet, also fake zipping her mouth.

"Good," says Isaac, looking intensely into their eyes. "Come with me."

Isaac leads Pip and Russet into the workshop, revealing the truth about Newton's tree and its special apples. He then opens

Newton's box to demonstrate the principles of Newton's apples. At first, they don't believe him, calling him a magician, a trickster, a street con-artist, but after experiencing the apples' force for themselves, they are immediate converts.

Pip and Russet are as excited as Isaac, and Isaac is delighted to have two new friends to play.

"Let's try the apples outside," suggests Isaac, grabbing a five-castor chair from beneath a workbench. "We'll use this chair."

Isaac takes the red apple. He wants to show Pip and Russet the potential power of Newton's apples. Sat in the chair in the middle of the courtyard, Isaac motions for Pip and Russet to stand back as if to witness a space rocket launch. He counts down - three, two, one and turns the red apple upside down.

Isaac flies into the air...but leaves the chair behind!

Pip and Russet are shocked to see him fly but can't help chuckling as they glance at the empty chair! Red-faced, Isaac comes back down to earth and runs into the workshop to fetch something to make him at one with the chair. He returns clutching a length of rope which he ties through the side arms, under the seat and over his lap, securing it with a double bow.

Giving Pip and Russet an embarrassed smile, Isaac counts down again before flying into the air...this time strapped to the chair!

"Three *chairs* for Isaac!" shout Pip and Russet, delighting in Isaac's success as they watch him move up and down as he controls the red apple's orientation, discovering that half a turn back places the forces in equilibrium - enabling him to hover and maintain a constant altitude. The centre of gravity is slightly off-kilter, tipping Isaac forward which he finds disconcerting, but corrects when he leans back and holds the apple closer.

They each have a go - Isaac briefing them carefully to avoid his mistakes. It's hilarious. Pip shows no fear and rockets himself three hundred feet into the air, coming back down to earth with the biggest grin you've ever seen! Russet is more cautious, flying upwards for three seconds before hovering like a hawk with a birds-eye-view of Ezer's grounds. She too comes back down to earth, fizzing and overflowing with excitement.

All three try the yellow *accelerator* apple, starting at one end of the courtyard and racing to the other end - the castors, struggling to keep up. Russet is more *stop-start*, flicking the apple back and forth like a games console joystick, but after three laps of the courtyard, she discovers her daredevil, and like Pip and Isaac, she judges her momentum to perfection, stopping six inches from the courtyard wall, screaming, "Hello, Wall! Pleased to meet you!"

They repeat this with the green *direction* apple, moving crablike across the courtyard, inversely moving their arms side to side, pretending to disco dance and change direction to the funky beat playing on Pip's smartphone. It's hysterical!

"After lunch, we'll combine all three!" says Isaac - everyone nodding their agreement. "Would you like to have lunch here?"

"We better go home for lunch," reply Pip and Russet, disappointed, "Mum will be expecting us!"

"No problem!" replies Isaac, also disappointed, "But hurry back, and remember, guys...*Rabbit Stew's* the word!"

17
Three bruised egos!

Ezer is yet to return. Isaac shrugs this off without concern other than that there is no prepared lunch!

Instead, Isaac gobbles down Ezer's breakfast he substituted earlier with Newton's apples. Unsure how to reheat, Isaac settles for cold *Eggs Benedict* sitting under a clear cloche - the apple smoke now vanished. It is skillfully crafted to resemble a Benedictine monk - a single poached egg, *bald head* with a ring of tempered truffle flavoured hollandaise, *hair* sits on a circular ham, *habit*, all placed on a thirteen-millimetre-thick circular muffin, *body*. It's still divine - despite the egg being on the rubbery side and the hollandaise sauce having the consistency of congealed custard!

The Chocolate Surprise is still warm in its insulated golden droplet and is an experience, Isaac will never tire.

Isaac enters the courtyard at the same time as Pip and Russet. They are all out of breath and keen to continue.

"How was lunch?" enquires Isaac, leading Pip and Russet into the workshop.

"Mum makes a mean *cheese on toast!*" replies Pip, proudly.

"She adds onion and apple to a whisked egg, seasons with salt and pepper, and a touch of chilli flake!" details Russet, "All toasted on a thirteen-millimetre *doorstop*. You have to try it, Isaac!"

Isaac is stunned by the familiarity of such detail. Not to be outdone, he pontificates over his Eggs Benedict, overlooking its temperature and any vow of silence to Ezer, intimately detailing his Benedictine monk!

"That sounds more like breakfast!" points out Pip.

"My Uncle said he'd be back by eleven," responds Isaac, wondering why certain foods better suit certain times of the day, "and he left no lunch - just my breakfast I neglected to eat earlier!"

"Why do you think he's late?" asks Russet, wondering why Isaac isn't more concerned.

"I'm sure he'll be back anytime soon!" replies Isaac with a reassuring smile, "So let's get cracking!"

Isaac, Pip and Russet swap ideas on how to combine the apples before Pip hits on a possibility.

"There's an old discarded tractor tyre in the far corner of the field," suggests Pip.

"It's massive!" reveals Russet, stretching out her hands to describe its diameter. "Slowly consumed by nature, but it's still salvageable!"

"And it's got holes in its central hub where we can attach ourselves!" enthuses Pip, closing his eyes to picture the wheel, and counting aloud with a circular moving pointed finger. "One, two, three, four, five holes!"

"Excellent!" decides Isaac, placing Newton's box under his arm and handing Pip three lengths of rope. "You show the way, Russet."

Sure enough, in the corner of the field, and not too far from the cow's water trough, is a large tractor tyre - long grass sprouting through its hub like an *eighties* haircut!

It's heavy. Far too heavy for three kids to lift, even if they all try from one side. It measures six feet in diameter and eighteen inches thick - its hub red and rust-coloured.

"There's only one thing for it!" concludes Isaac.

"And what's that?" asks Pip, placing his hands in his pockets.

"We have to fly it out of there!" replies Isaac, motioning like a whimsically flying butterfly.

Messing about in the courtyard is one thing, flying an enormous tractor tyre from the corner of a cow filed is quite another!

Isaac looks at Pip and Russet, clocking their coloured apparel and proclaims, "That's easy - Pip you take charge of the green apple and *direction*, wearing your green hoody. Russet you take charge of the yellow apple and *acceleration*, wearing your yellow hoody, and I'll take charge of the red apple and *lift*, wearing my red top!"

After further deliberation, Pip and Russet agree to swap hoodies and flying responsibility.

"I'm a little scared of speed," admits Russet, pulling the green hoody over her head before declaring with a wry smile, "but I know where I'm going in life and I can steer us carefully in the direction we need to go!"

Pip and Russet climb onto the tractor wheel and sit on the outer black tyre, placing their feet on the inner hub. Isaac takes a step back - something doesn't look right.

"I think we should sit on the hub with our backs supporting each other and our feet on the outer black tyre," directs Isaac, twizzling his finger as if stirring a cup of tea. "That way, we can look outwards and see where we're going!"

Pip and Russet turn around, acknowledging the common sense in his proposal. Isaac ties Pip and Russet to the tractor tyre, weaving the rope through the hub holes and around their laps. He grabs the box, climbs onboard and similarly ties himself. Opening Newton's box, Isaac hands Pip the yellow apple, Russet the green apple and takes the red apple for himself. Unsure where to put the box, but reluctant to leave it behind, Isaac wedges it between him and Pip.

The nervousness is real - they can feel each other's hearts beating ten to the dozen and pulsating through their backs like automated massage chairs.

It's not every day you use magic apples to fly a discarded tractor tyre from the corner of a cow field - it's not every day you use magic apples to fly...full stop!

Isaac, Pip and Russet discuss tactics, agreeing on *SPONDOOLY* as an alarm call, for no other reason than it sounds good!

"Every *ship* must have a name!" shouts Russet, in danger of adopting delay tactics for their departure, "It's good luck!"

Agreeing on an alarm call is easy compared with agreeing on a *ship's* name! They're still discussing after twenty minutes!

"Unless anyone disagrees," suggests Isaac, decisively and keen to progress, "Let's call it *NEWTON'S APPLES.*"

Silence settles it. But then a discussion about christening prevails. Instead of champagne, they clink apples and nominate Russet, as the female, to proclaim, "I christen thee, NEWTON'S APPLES!"

Finally, the fun can begin. Isaac turns his red apple upside down. The tyre begins to lift on one side - caked in set mud on the other. Then it dislodges, and like an elastic band, it shoots into the air, throwing Isaac, Pip and Russet into disarray and almost into the branches of an overhanging English oak!

Russet intuitively turns her apple to the right attempting to steer the tyre to the right, forgetting its opposite effect, and heads straight for the woods. Luckily her razor-sharp reflexes avoid disaster, and she steers right, as she turns her green apple left!

Isaac turns his red apple back a quarter turn to hold the tyre fifteen feet above the ground. Russet returns her green apple upright. They remain static, hovering silently like a puck on an air hockey table. The cud-chewing cows stare indifferently - neither confused nor excited, lowering their heads to tear another mouthful of grass.

"We did it!" exclaims Isaac, wishing he could see the look in his colleagues' faces.

"We're flying!" shouts Russet, realising her over-exuberance and hearing Isaac shushing, whispering, "We're flying!"

"We don't want your Mum hearing!" states Isaac.

"Exactly," adds Pip, "Imagine explaining this to her!"

Russet agrees.

"Right, Pip," continues Isaac, "it's up to you now. Let's go to the other side of the field!"

Isaac instantly recognises his vagueness as they head off in Pip's direction back to the woods and not as he had hoped, to the far end of the field by the driveway and the gated front entrance.

"Go *right,* Russet!" orders Isaac, raising his voice at Russet as she turns left, *"Right,* I said!"

"I turned *left* to go *right,"* answers Russet, becoming agitated with Isaac. "Maybe it's your orders that are wrong!"

"Then *left!"* responds Isaac, equally agitated, "Turn *right* to go *left!"*

Russet does as she's instructed and turns left - her left! Facing away from each other disorientates their sense of direction - they're heading for Ezer's workshop. Russet averts a collision, turning her apple *left* to turn *right!*

Pip, is confused, unable to see where he's going, and pushes his yellow apple away from him, accelerating out of control.

"Slow down, Pip!" screams Isaac, "Turn *right,* Russet!"

It's not long before it's pandemonium and they're darting around the field like an out-of-control stunt kite, moving up and down, side to side and back and forth. Isaac wobbles his apple attempting to see where he's going, Pip pulls back then pushes forwards to speed up and slow down, and Russet turns left and right to go right and left!

They fly over the driveway and narrowly miss Ezer in La Dauphine - returning home and innocently whistling the tune to *Miss You* by the *Rolling Stones!*

Ezer screeches to a stop to hear three kids scream, "SPONDOOLY!" and crash land into the manicured lawn laid to the front of the house, daisy-cutting and rose budding in the process - bouncing three times before planting one foot from a mature beech...its trunk matching NEWTON'S APPLES girth but outmatching it on so many other levels!

Isaac, Pip and Russet are speechless, rubbing their heads after banging together on impact!

"Ahh, my head!" shrieks Russet, rocking to and fro as she rubs, "I've got two of those cartoon bumps on either side of my head!"

"Me, too!" yelps Pip, further exaggerating, "Like billy goat horns!"

"That was a close call!" declares Isaac, seeing Ezer approach. "Quick. Put your apples back in the box. Ezer's coming!"

Isaac retrieves the box and collects each apple, thanking his lucky stars that the box survives. He closes the box just as Ezer arrives.

"Goodness me! Are you OK? You missed me by the closest of margins!"

enquires Ezer with a concerned expression.

"We're OK!" replies Isaac, trying to appear normal! "Just a few bumps and three bruised egos!"

"You could have been killed - we could have all been killed! Who are your friends, Isaac?

And how, and why are you flying an over-sized tractor tyre? Explain!"

probes Ezer as his responsibility as Isaac's guardian replaces his relief that no one is seriously hurt.

"This is Pip, and this is Russet," introduces Isaac, pointing to each in turn. "They're brother and sister and live in the cottage on the other side of the woods by the cow field."

"Hello, Mr Strangeman," quietly greets Pip, echoed by Russet - both unable to look Ezer in the eye. "We're pleased to meet you!"

Ezer says nothing, but nods which only Isaac sees. Isaac thinks through his explanation - reluctant to *grass* on his new friends or detail their apple scrumping.

"It's a long story," begins Isaac as if he should be checking if Ezer is sitting comfortably! "It all began with me discovering this triangular wooden box under Newton's tree in the orchard. It has the initials I.N. engraved on the badge which I believe stand for *Isaac Newton*. The box contains three different coloured apples - magic apples...each one relating to Newton's Laws of Motion and able to induce lift, acceleration and direction."

Isaac offers up the box to Ezer. Ezer takes the box and studies it, initially saying nothing until he begins to shake his head and say,

"I have read about
these magic apples, but wrote
them off as fiction!
I believe you. Let's
get back to the workshop,
and you can show me!"

Ezer helps to untie Isaac, Pip and Russet. All four up-turn the tyre and wheel it back to the workshop - past La Dauphine...waiting patiently to be collected later.

Ezer shakes Pip and Russet by the hand which immediately puts them at ease, and able to trust Isaac's description of him as *misunderstood* and *one in a million!*

18

The power of invention!

After leaning the wheel against the courtyard wall, Isaac, Pip and Russet follow Ezer into the workshop. They stand either side of Ezer as he places Newton's box on the bench. Like Isaac, Ezer can't decipher how it opens.

"Let me show you, Ezer," offers Isaac, sliding the box towards him. "It's easy when you know how! You push these two areas here, and it opens like so....pushing a wedge forwards which disengages the internal lock like so...allowing you to open the lid like so. There you go!"

Ezer's face lights up as he peruses the coloured apples and the brilliance of the polished brass rhombus open box, exclaiming,

"These apples are the
most beautiful things I've seen -
like fine jewellery!"

Isaac demonstrates the principles of each apple with input from Pip and Russet - now experts on the yellow and green apples!

"You've discovered self-
powered lift, direction and
acceleration!

No motors, engines,
fuel, electricity.
It's free energy!"

excites Ezer, placing his arms around Isaac, Pip and Russet, continuing,

"We should convert the
golf cart to run by these three
magical apples!"

"What about the souped-up motor you've just got?" asks Isaac.

"Don't worry about
that! We're going to create
a flying machine!"

"It's going to be better than a discarded tractor wheel!" declares Pip, looking wide-eyed at the metallic gold golf cart body hanging in the spray booth.

"Exactly!" adds Isaac, pointing to the three-wheeled chassis, "Everyone will be facing forwards in the same direction!"

"No more confusion!" chirps Russet, giving Isaac a smile and shaking her head, "When left means left and right means right!"

"Precisely, Russet," responds Isaac, smiling and raising his eyebrows, "When left means left and right means right!"

"We can design three
steering wheels - one each for red,
yellow and green seats!"

suggests Ezer, uncovering the golf cart seats for Pip and Russet.

"Do you think we can design the green direction steering wheel to turn the apple *left* when we want to turn *right* and turn *right* when we want to turn *left*?" asks Russet, hopefully,

"Like on a boat," points out Isaac, "where the rudder turns in the opposite direction to the steering wheel!"

"Yeah! Just like that!" agrees Russet, "It messes with your mind to recondition your brain!"

"All is possible
if we put our minds to it!
Called problem-solving!"

enthuses Ezer, excited to work with three inquisitive minds.

"The power of invention!" cries Pip, standing under the clear dome suspended from the ceiling - the sound reverberating and echoing as he continues, "Where there's no such word as *no!*"

"Where there's a will, there's
a way! It boils down to how
deep are your pockets!?"

replies Ezer, pulling his pockets inside out like two puppy dog ears! Declaring,

"I have very deep
pockets, but more than that - I
love spending money!"

"He has and does!" confirms Isaac. "Did you know he's the inventor of *Kerfluffle?*"

"The belly button de-fluffer?" enquires Russet.

"The very same!" replies Isaac as Ezer modestly lowers his gaze.

"Wow!" exclaims Pip, "I go through three *Kerfluffles* a week!"

"That's why I have deep
pockets. Simple solution
to a daily need!"

says Ezer, grinning like a Cheshire cat, and handing Isaac, Pip and Russet a black workshop coat, each embroidered on the back with a golden flying dolphin. Somehow, inconceivably quickly, Ezer has changed out of his driving gear - the gear he wore to pick up Isaac, and into a similar black workshop coat, a yellow shirt, blue denim jeans and tan coloured steel toed work shoes. His hair is sticking up like a mad professor - he's wearing a pair of green rimmed spectacles, and a small steel ruler protrudes from his chest pocket!

Ezer leads them through a *brainstorming* session, itemising ideas and requirements on a whiteboard - Isaac scribbling his contribution in red pen, Pip in yellow and Russet in green. The modifications to the existing golf cart are mainly centred around a *steering wheel* to be placed in front of each seat. Ezer charges Isaac, Pip and Russet with responsibility for the function and specification of their respective steering wheel. He gives each a pad and some pens and encourages them to produce something truly original and worthy of The Flying Dolphin!

Isaac, Pip and Russet struggle to create anything other than a conventional steering wheel with an apple container mounted to its face! Ezer intervenes, grabbing a piece of tubing,

"Who's heard of the
Cartesian coordinate
system? ...Isaac? ...Pip?"

"Is that the system that places coordinates on different axis?" enquires Russet, agitated that Ezer looked to the boys first!

"Yes. Very good, Russet!
X, Y and Z axis
to define a point!"

begins Ezer, turning the whiteboard around to draw three axes and mark them with X, Y and Z.

"We've used them in maths to plot charts and basic algorithms," offers Isaac, keen to contribute.

"More than defining
points in space - these three axes
define direction!

X is *front to back*,
Y is *side to side*, leaving
Z for *up and down!*"

"So, axis-X is me!" offers Pip, putting his hand up as if he's in class, "The yellow apple. Front to back. Acceleration!"

"And axis-Y is me!" follows Russet, also putting her hand up halfway before lowering awkwardly, "The green apple. Side to side. Direction!"

"And axis-Z is me!" deduces Isaac, by merit not by default! "The red apple. Up and Down. Lift!"

"Precisely! If we
design a geared tube to turn
each apple then we
make yellow as Y,
red as Z and green as X
- all with sliding sleeves!"

details Ezer, drawing his idea and demonstrating with the piece of tubing. He holds the tube like a relay baton for X, a horizontal water-ski handle for Y and a vertical flagpole for Z.

"And each sliding sleeve can be the colour of the apple," suggests Russet, building on Ezer's logic. Ezer nods, adding,

"Each coloured sleeve has
click and leave positions and
is easy to view!"

Isaac, Pip and Russet are beside themselves. One minute they're flying on a tractor tyre, or rather crash-landing into the front lawn and narrowly missing Ezer! The next, they're designing their own flying machine!

Ezer sits at the three-dimensional computer, inputting data and pre-set dimensions. He doesn't have to worry about linking the steering bar to wheels or shafts - so long as it revolves one of Newton's apples and is easy to operate!

Each steering bar has a vertical post that attaches to the chassis through the floor and is positioned centrally to each seat. The post has a right-angle bend onto which mounts the apple holding sleeve with its integral gearing plate. The apple inserts and removes by rotating an outer sleeve to reveal a spring-loaded claw. The claw opens to place each apple on a single point and closes to hold each stem.

Each bar is identical. It is three hundred and thirty-three millimetres long, sixty-six millimetres in diameter and sprayed matt black. The outer sliding sleeve has a five-millimetre thickness, is one hundred and eleven millimetres long, and wraps around the steering bar by two hundred and forty degrees. It *clicks and stays* either end and in a central neutral position by pressing small opposing buttons contained on the sleeve which engage with an internal mechanism.

Then each bar has a different rear gearing module depending on its apple and orientation. The vertical red bar comes out of the back and attaches directly to the apple turning gear plate. The horizontal green apple also comes out of the back and attaches directly to the gearing plate, but the internal gearing is turned through ninety degrees with an extra feature to correct the opposing steering. There is also an additional button to reverse this when the flying machine needs to travel in *reverse*. The horizontal yellow bar comes out of the back but goes downwards to connect to the apple steering gear plate through a side mounted gear module. Ezer also designs a feature to allow the yellow bar to rotate through thirty degrees when accessing the apple. Ingenious!

Ezer sends the data to the three-dimensional printers and automatic milling machines to be made overnight. They will colour and assemble the parts first thing in the morning.

"Look at the time, Russet!" shrieks Pip, "It's nearly eight o'clock!"

"OMG!" exclaims Russet, "We better get back. Mum will be tearing her hair out!"

"Why don't you stay the night?" suggests Isaac, looking at Ezer for approval, "There's plenty of room, and we can have a BBQ!"

"We'll ask, but we can't promise!" replies Pip, removing his workshop coat. Russet does the same. Pip and Russet head home while Ezer and Isaac finish setting the machines and tidy the workshop.

"However busy
you are - you must make time to
tidy the workshop!"

remarks Ezer, replacing tools and sweeping the floor. Just as Ezer and Isaac head for the door, Pip and Russet burst through, yelling,

"We can't stay the night, but we can stay for the BBQ!"

"Fantastic!" shouts Isaac, high-fiving Pip and Russet, "Ezer makes the meanest star burger!"

Copernicus shadows Isaac, Pip and Russet around to the rear garden. Ezer arrives, having changed inconceivably quickly into Chef Strangeman and begins cooking!

Pip and Russet leave around ten o'clock after star-burgers, Chocolate Surprises and three twenty-minute games of SNOOKANOVA.

Tomorrow can't come soon enough!

19

Bramley apple pie!

Isaac can't sleep even though he desperately needs to replenish his energy for another action-packed day. Restless and resigned to being wide awake, rather than lie staring into space, Isaac heads for the domed turret to stare into space!

Ezer mentioned over dinner that Jupiter and Venus are orbiting close to earth and that they are worth observing. Isaac gazes into the night sky and spots the planets before rotating the dome and targeting the telescope. He finds Venus, shining bright and much closer than the first time he viewed it with Mr Mount and the school astronomy club.

"What a beautiful planet," remarks Isaac as if conversing with a companion. "No wonder the Romans named their *god of love* after her...or was it the other way around? Latter-day astrologers name the planet after the Roman god! God knows!" concludes Isaac, chuckling at his own joke!

As Isaac swivels the telescope on its mount to see if he can locate Jupiter without resetting the dome window, he stops dead - shocked by the vision before him. It's a *nebula supernova* - the rare occurrence of an exploding stellar event! Isaac is witnessing the implosion of a star from millions of years ago as its *gravity* to *radiation* balance loses equilibrium! The gravitational *pull* outweighs the radiation *push*, causing the entire mass of the star's core and its surrounding matter to disappear in on itself and leave a *black hole* - black because not even light can escape! These highly infrequent phenomena are difficult to predict. Isaac marvels at this wonder of the universe...in his pyjamas...when he should be sleeping! He revisits the telescopic view several times, revelling in its spectacle and his fortunate timing.

As the sun rises, the view weakens and becomes difficult to define. Isaac sees this as a good time to get ready for the new day. He hopes Ezer is an early riser, so they can share his news and resume the workshop activities as soon as possible.

Isaac dresses in the same green combat trousers and yellow baseball boots but dons a clean blue and white striped sailor's top, a brown leather flying jacket and a red baseball cap emblazoned with a five-pointed yellow star on its peak. He runs downstairs in search of Ezer but is disappointed when Ezer is nowhere to be found. Thinking Ezer is sleeping, Isaac sits in the front hall, stroking Copernicus and waits patiently for him to stir.

The distinctive roar of a petrol engine gets louder and louder, revving and changing gears as it screeches to a halt outside the front door. Isaac runs outside to find Ezer disembarking from a yellow *beach buggy* with all-terrain tyres, two red seats and a green stripe running front to back. Ezer is dressed all in black - a turtleneck pullover, black jeans, black biker boots and a black leather jacket...his ginger red hair wrapped in a black bandana.

"Morning, Ezer!" greets Isaac, unsure why Ezer is up so early and rolling around in a *sixties* off-road vehicle. Ezer skips formalities, outbursting,

"I've been watching a
nebula supernova!
Birth of a black hole!

An exploding star
with a flash of light brighter
than the brightest light!"

"You've taken the words right out of my mouth!" replies Isaac appearing to pour cold water over Ezer's news. "I couldn't sleep, so I looked for Venus and Jupiter through Newton's telescope, as you recommended, and then it happened...in front of my eyes! It was amazing - out of this world! Where did you see it, Ezer?"

"From my state-of-the-
art observatory up
by Gravity Falls!"

replies Ezer, stretching a large yawn and entering the front door,

"Glad you saw this rare
event. I thought you missed it.
Let's have some breakfast!

What time will your friends
arrive? I can't wait to start -
there's so much to do!"

"I'm not sure," replies Isaac, "they mentioned they might have to go shopping with their mother, but they'd try to get out of it..."

Ezer says nothing and heads for the kitchen. Isaac and Copernicus follow. No sooner does Isaac pull himself up onto a kitchen stool than Ezer returns from the side room, dressed as Chef Strangeman. Isaac wants to quiz Ezer about his speedy changing but thinks better of it, remembering his father's resonant phrase - *he's one in a million!*

"I feel like pancakes
with apple and blackberries
I picked this morning!

Star or dolphin-shaped
pancakes? I don't know 'bout you,
but I am starving!"

enthuses Ezer as he takes out a clear tub of blackberries from his black leather jacket pocket. They are still glistening with mildew.

"Perhaps three of each!" answers Isaac, watching Ezer meticulously prepare the pancake mix, "We have a busy day ahead!"

Ezer has a special griddle with dolphin and star-shaped indents, heated to exactly fifty-five degrees Celsius, and into which he pours five-millimetre-thick batter. Flipping onto a warmed pentagonal black ceramic plate, Ezer adds red apple compote to one pair of star and dolphin pancakes, yellow apple compote to another pair and green apple compote to the final pair. He tops each pancake with three bulbous blackberries and passes the finished plate to Isaac together with a gold knife and fork, elegantly designed and engraved with a flying dolphin.

"Thank you, Ezer," says Isaac, licking his lips. "They look like stars and constellations in the midnight sky!"

"Fill your *black hole* for
an explosion of taste like
a *supernova!*"

jokes Ezer, handing Isaac a Chocolate Surprise.

"I see what you did!" replies Isaac, taking his first bite of a star-shaped red apple concoction. "Good one, Ezer!"

A blackberry explodes into tiny pieces as its drupelets simultaneously burst to fill Isaac's mouth with sweet-flavoured fruit juice, immediately complemented with aromatic apple before the savoury taste of pancake pans around his mouth and cakes his tongue in a melting mixture of seventh heaven!

Isaac says it all by finishing all six pancakes before Ezer starts his first!

After breakfast, Ezer changes inconceivably quickly back into yesterday's workshop gear and leads Isaac over to the workshop. It's eight o'clock.

Ezer retrieves the individual parts from the machines and prepares them for spraying. He shows Isaac how to etch, prime and top coat each element. It's nearly ten o'clock before Pip and Russet tap three times on the workshop door.

"Hi, guys!" welcomes Isaac, high-fiving Pip and Russet as they enter, holding a red cake tin and wearing their yellow and green hoodies, "Good timing. We've finished all the spraying and ready to start assembling!"

"Mum insisted we bring some morning tea!" informs Russet, placing the red tin on the bench and lifting the lid.

"Her famous *Bramley* apple pie!" adds Pip, taking off his rucksack and pulling out four paper plates and some picnic cutlery. "Nothing beats Mum's *Bramley* apple pie!"

Ezer looks up, intrigued by such a declaration. He wanders over, saying hello to Pip and Russet and waits to be served. Russet cuts four slices and dishes out while Pip hands everyone a portion.

"It's very good!" compliments Isaac, enquiring if there is any more.

Pip and Russet devour theirs with proud smiles and told-you-so nods!

Ezer takes bite after bite, smelling the *bouquet* and pushing every mouthful to the four corners of his mouth to taste its sweetness, acidity, and vintage like a sommelier tastes a fine wine. There's something familiar about it, but he can't put his finger on it - it's on the tip of his tongue!

Just as he finishes the last mouthful, a single knock sounds loudly on the workshop door. Everyone looks at each other expecting the other to suggest who it might be. Isaac puts down his plate and walks over to open the door. A woman with black hair, deep green eyes and bright red lipstick smiles at Isaac.

"You must be Isaac," she begins, offering her hand for Isaac to shake, "I'm Theresa Bramley. Pip and Russet's mother!"

"Pleased to meet you, Mrs Bramley," responds Isaac, nervously as if she's caught them red-handed, doing something they're not supposed to be doing! "I've heard a lot about you, and we're just sampling your terrific apple pie!"

"That's too kind!" she replies, reaching into the pocket of her bright yellow mac. "Pip forgot his inhaler, and he must have it in case of an emergency."

"Come in, Mrs Bramley and give it to him yourself," replies Isaac, stepping back to usher in Mrs Bramley, "You can meet my Uncle."

"Please call me, Theresa," she insists, "or *Trezer* as Pip and Russet nickname me!"

"Hi, Mum," greet Pip and Russet - Pip tutting and realising his oversight.

"Trezer," begins Isaac, gesturing to Ezer, "This is my Uncle, Ezer!"

Ezer and Trezer say nothing. They both have a look of complete shock as if they've seen the ghost of Christmas past!

"Trezer and Ezer!" remarks Pip, giggling and pointing, "How funny is that!"

"I knew I'd tasted
that apple pie before, but
couldn't work out where!"

begins Ezer, staring intensely.

"Is it really you, Ezer?" replies Trezer, staring back with equal intensity, "What am I saying? Of course, it's you! Who else speaks in haiku!"

Isaac, Pip and Russet give each other puzzled exchanges.

"You haven't changed. Still
as beautiful as ever!
How long has it been?...at least ten years..."

continues Ezer, falling out of haiku for a moment as he looks Trezer up and down. He puts a clenched fist to his mouth and clears his throat as if to reset and regain his composure.

"Nearly thirteen years!" answers Trezer, "You haven't changed either, Ezer. Still looking good!"

Ezer blushes as red as his ginger red hair! Trezer and Ezer suddenly realise they owe Isaac, Pip and Russet an explanation.

"We were good friends many years ago," informs Trezer, averting her gaze away from Ezer, "before the success of Ker**fluf**fle!"

Ezer shifts uncomfortably from one foot to the next, allowing Trezer to continue,

"We were close, but Ezer was so wrapped up in his inventions - obsessed with belly buttons and bits of fluff! There was no time or space for me. So I left and moved elsewhere," relays Trezer, looking again at Ezer, who is now staring at the floor. "I thought you'd moved away, Ezer? I had no idea you still lived here when I bought the cottage last year. I thought *Gravity Falls* was a hotel or a country club, and when Pip and Russet mentioned their new friend, Isaac - staying with his *Uncle*, I had no idea that it was YOU!"

"Tried to find you. It
was like you disappeared off
the face of the earth!"

states Ezer, looking at Trezer then changing the subject,

"Why don't you come for
dinner tonight? Pip, Russet
and you together!"

"I'd like that!" replies Trezer, smiling and relieved to lighten the mood. "We can catch up on old times!"

Isaac, Pip and Russet are delighted. It means they can spend more time together!

"Can I bring anything?" asks Trezer, heading for the door.

"Just yourself and a
jumper in case it gets cold!
Look forward to it!"

replies Ezer, escorting Trezer to the door.

"What are you making?" enquires Trezer, looking at the triangular chassis. "Pip and Russet won't tell me!"

"Nothing really!
A souped-up golf cart for the
kids to drive around!"

responds Ezer, giving Isaac, Pip and Russet a knowing glance before bidding Trezer goodbye!

20
Good luck to all who fly in her!

Isaac, Pip and Russet help Ezer to assemble their respective vertical posts and geared direction sliding bars. Everything goes together like clockwork. They use three tennis balls to test the mechanisms instead of Newton's apples for fear of flying around the workshop and causing untold damage! Ezer hammers a nail into each tennis ball to mimic the stem.

Ezer bolts each post to the triangular chassis which now supports a black rubber circular floor. They place each seat in position and bolt them to the chassis through the floor - the red seat at the front, the yellow and green seats behind and in that order when viewed looking forwards.

Ezer summons all-hands-on-deck to move the metallic gold body into position. Made from glass fibre, it weighs a lot less than it looks and lifts over the seats and vertical steering posts with relative ease - locating onto three chassis corner fixings. Ezer tightens with the correct *torque* - enough to ensure the fixings do not become loose, but not too tight as to damage or make them impossible to remove. The body has a complete ring of LED lights around the outer circumference embedded into a black rubber strip for protection. A single LED flush mounted headlight is centrally positioned below the strip. The front wheel locks or unlocks for manoeuvrability.

Isaac, Pip and Russet climb into their seats, adjust the *driving* position and connect the three-point safety harness. While they're sitting, Ezer grabs the ceiling hoist controls and lowers the clear domed roof into position, securing the cantilever hinge at the rear and checking the manual sidelocks.

The look on Isaac, Pip and Russet's faces is a picture of complete joy and happiness! It fills Ezer with a sense of paternal pride!

Ezer instructs Isaac how to open the roof. It requires little force to rotate it rearwards for cockpit access. Ezer then runs to the far end of the workshop and returns clutching three yellow and black bicycle helmets, each with integrated wasp-eye visors and illuminated displays.

Happy with everything, Ezer helps them out of The Flying Dolphin to add the final touches. While Isaac, Pip and Russet assist each other in adjusting their helmets - hiding their nerves behind excited smiles, Ezer unwraps a polished chrome flying dolphin badge with *The Flying Dolphin* subtly engraved down its back and attaches it to the body's *nose*.

Isaac, Pip and Russet run through the sliding bar positions and their corresponding directions - Isaac and Russet teasing each other about yesterday's cow field debacle!

Meanwhile, Ezer suspends a chain from the ceiling hoist and guides it to the front right side of The Flying Dolphin. Grabbing a bottle of champagne from the small fridge, he fixes it to the ceiling hoist chain with gold duct tape, yelling,

"Russet. Please, can you
ceremoniously name
this ship for good luck!"

Russet pulls back the green bottle with its gold foil top and bright red label, and releases it like a skittles bowling game, declaring, "I name this airship, *The Flying Dolphin*. Good luck to all who fly in her!"

The champagne smashes into a metal strip, temporarily added to the body by Ezer for protection! A tirade of bubbles showers the body in a cloak of fizz.

"Three cheers!" shouts Isaac with everyone joining, "Hip, hip - hooray! Hip, hip - hooray! Hip, hip - hooray!"

Ezer connects a pulling device to the front wheel and guides The Flying Dolphin out into the courtyard - opening both doors to facilitate. He wheels it to the centre, disconnects the pulling device and locks the front wheel. It's ready for its maiden flight!

Isaac returns to the workshop and picks up the box of Newton's apples and carries it back to the courtyard like an Olympic official bringing the ceremony medals. Ezer takes the box while Isaac, Pip and Russet retake their positions - Isaac in the red seat, Pip in the yellow seat and Russet in the green seat. They secure their harness and make last-minute adjustments to their helmets. Pip looks to his sister and offers his hand. Russet grips his hand and wishes him good luck. Pip reciprocates.

"It's been great knowing you!" jokes Isaac, trying to diffuse the tension before realising his insensitivity, adding, "Just kidding! Everything's going to be fine!"

"Once we're up!" replies Pip, playfully kicking Isaac's seat.

"There's not a lot we can hit once we're up!" exclaims Russet, trying to remain positive, "But it's the getting up and down - the take-off and landing that worries me!"

"Open your apple covers. I suggest a test to check everything!"

instructs Ezer, opening the box and inserting each Newton apple into the correct steering post and double checking!

"A return tour to
Gravity Falls then land in
rear garden for lunch!"

"Sounds like a great plan, Ezer!" exclaims Isaac, closing his apple cover and preparing for take-off. "Maybe some of your *Tricolour* sandwiches to mark the occasion would go down well, Ezer!"

Pip and Russet close their apple covers and lower the clear dome roof, securing the side latches. Ezer retreats to lean against the workshop wall. Isaac assumes the captain's responsibilities, sitting in the front seat and operating the essential flying function. He pretends to be a movie actor, cross-checking,

"Left door latch, Pip?"

"Closed!" replies Pip, thinking he's saying the right thing!

"Say, *check!*" corrects Isaac, searching for authenticity, "Not, *closed!* Start again!"

"Left door latch, Pip?" repeats Isaac.

"Check!" replies Pip with a dismissive shake of his head - invisible to Isaac!

"Right door latch, Russet?"

"Check!" replies Russet, giving Pip a supportive glance.

"Apples, locked and loaded? Pip? Russet?" continues Isaac.

"Check. Check," answer Pip and Russet, beginning to enjoy the role play.

"Everyone good to go? Pip? Russet?" concludes Isaac.

"Check. Check." answer Pip and Russet - Pip adding, "And Isaac - everything good to go?"

"Check!" replies Isaac, counting down, "Three, two, one. Take-off!"

Isaac moves his red sleeve to the *up* position. The Flying Dolphin accelerates upwards, leaving Ezer to wave and holler frantically!

Ezer programmes an altimeter to display beside the speedometer in their helmet visors. Initially is reads in feet, too fast for the eye to keep up. Isaac presses a button on the side of his helmet and changes it to read in metres. When they reach sixty-six metres, he lowers his red sleeve back to the central position. The Flying Dolphin stops accelerating and hovers at a constant altitude.

The Flying Dolphin has a three-degree angle pitch towards the front. Ezer sets this deliberately to mimic an aeroplane where three degrees provides enough lift to maintain constant altitude relative to its airspeed.

"We need to turn ninety degrees to the right and accelerate forwards, following the woods to the top of the hill," outlines Isaac, pointing to Gravity Falls, hidden from view, "So, Russet when I give the command, turn right...and that's right - not left to go right!"

"Yes, I know, Isaac!" replies Russet, gripping her green sleeve. "Just give the order!"

"Right, Russet!" orders Isaac.

"Check!" responds Russet, moving her green sleeve to the right and back again when facing in the correct direction. There is an electronic display in the visor. It reads north by northeast.

"Straight ahead, Pip!" orders Isaac.

"Check!" responds Pip, sliding his yellow sleeve forwards and accelerating up the hill.

The speedometer races upwards like a souped-up sports car. In no time at all, they're travelling at sixty-six miles an hour...and increasing!

"STOP!" shouts Isaac, seeing Gravity Falls pass by to their right. "We've gone too far!"

"You've got to give more warning!" responds Pip, sliding his yellow sleeve back to the middle, and becoming frustrated with Isaac's commands. "We don't know where Gravity Falls is...are!"

Now knowing where he's going, Pip puts The Flying Dolphin into reverse and backs up, coming to a stop in line with Gravity Falls as he moves the yellow sleeve back to the middle.

"Brilliant, Pip!" remarks Russet, staring at Gravity Falls in all its splendour below.

"Yes, brilliant, Pip!" encourages Isaac, keen not to appear bossy or unreasonable. "There she blows. Gravity Falls!"

Russet turns her green sleeve to the right. Pip anticipates this and moves his yellow sleeve forwards. Isaac simultaneously lowers his red sleeve. All three return their sleeves to bring The Flying Dolphin to a stop, hovering ten feet above the pool at the bottom of Gravity Falls - covering The Flying Dolphin in a fine spray.

Isaac tells Pip and Russet about his adventures flying off Gravity Falls in an underwater dolphin and how they can do this one day - Pip and Russet hanging on every word.

"We need windscreen wipers!" observes Russet as the spray turns into drips, turns into streaks of water. "I can hardly see!"

"Good point!" notes Isaac, "Let's go and have lunch and catch up with Ezer. At least it's a nice day, and the water will soon dry."

They agree to make a few loops around the top of Gravity Falls before returning. Isaac points out the rail for The Angry Wasp, but it's so well camouflaged, Pip and Russet can't see it!

Ezer's state-of-the-art observatory is mounted on a small knoll at the top of the hill and painted green to blend in with its surroundings.

With every flying loop, Isaac, Pip and Russet hone their sleeve control skills, anticipating and complementing each other's moves. Isaac doesn't need to keep giving orders!

They land on the rear lawn - a little heavier than Isaac had planned, or Pip and Russet had wanted, hoping to show Ezer how much they have improved since yesterday's near miss!

Ezer jogs over with Copernicus on his heels - helping to unlatch the side locks and open the clear dome roof.

"How was it? Did The
Flying Dolphin perform, or
were there some problems?"

enquires Ezer before they've had a chance to take stock.

"It was AMAZING!" scream Isaac, Pip and Russet, removing their helmets and ruffling their hair.

"We need wipers!" remarks Russet - Ezer nods.

"Let's have some lunch, and we'll tell you all about it," suggests Isaac, spying a plate full of Tricolour sandwiches and Chocolate Surprises.

Ezer can't get a word in edgeways over lunch as Isaac, Pip and Russet talk ten to the dozen and rave about the maiden flight! They're so consumed with the excitement of free energy powered motion, Isaac, Pip and Russet wolf down Ezer's Tricolour sandwiches without any comment or an ounce of attention!

Ezer doesn't mind - seeing the kids full up on *the food of life* is all the gratitude he needs.

"Let's go again!" excites Russet, tasting Ezer's Chocolate Surprise and stopping to exclaim, "OMG, this is the best drink I've ever had! Can this day get any better!?"

Everyone concurs and heads for The Flying Dolphin. Ezer hands over a hamper of chilled water and three bags of his apple flavoured fudge.

Isaac, Pip and Russet spend the afternoon flying here, there and everywhere, climbing higher over villages to avoid detection, and dipping lower over lakes and fields - swooping and swooning as they go. They determine that if they all lean when turning, The Flying Dolphin tips for a better view. They practice landing onto designated targets and get dizzy, spinning around and around.

Isaac, Pip and Russet have so much fun - they lose track of time. It's nearly seven o'clock.

As they land back into the courtyard, coming back over the cow field, Trezer double takes as she makes her way over for dinner!

21
Yes, a UFO!

"Hello, Trezer! Please
come through. I thought we'd eat out
side this evening!"

greets Ezer, opening the front door and leading Trezer through to the rear garden. Ezer is dressed in a white dinner jacket, white dinner shirt with a green cummerbund and red bow tie, and smart black trousers with a golden silk side stripe. His shoes are black patent leather, reflecting everywhere he goes. Trezer wears a little black dress with matching kitten heel shoes. Her hair is clipped up at the back and her gold necklace, encrusted with emeralds, glistens in the evening sun, complementing her deep red lipstick. She has a red shawl following Ezer's suggestion.

"You look very nice.
Is that the necklace I gave
you when we first met?"

compliments Ezer, trying hard not to blush.

"Yes, it is, Ezer…well remembered…and you look very nice, too! Thank you for inviting me," replies Trezer handing him a bottle. "Just a bottle of my fermented apple juice for you. I recall your weakness for anything apple!"

Isaac, Pip and Russet enter the rear garden through the adjoining courtyard side wall after *parking* The Flying Dolphin and covering it with a red sheet.

"Hi, Mum!" shout Pip and Russet, "Sorry we didn't get back home to change and come with you, but time flies when you're enjoying yourself!"

"Hi, Trezer!" adds Isaac, hoping to help Pip and Russet's alibi, "We've been in the workshop all day working on the golf cart!"

Trezer gives Isaac, Pip and Russet a half-hearted nod as if something doesn't quite add up. She looks at Ezer and steps back in amazement - Ezer is now dressed as Chef Strangeman and carrying a tray of steaks and kebabs!

"How did you change so fast?" begins Trezer, looking at Isaac, Pip and Russet then back to Ezer. "Don't answer! I remember now!" she continues, refocusing on Isaac's words, "I wanted to ask you about something strange that happened to me on my way over."

"How do you like your steak? Rare, medium or well done? They are sirloin!"

Ezer asks Trezer, looking to change the subject. He repeats the question to Isaac, Pip and Russet who are helping themselves to fresh apple juice from three jugs marked *red apple*, *golden apple* and *green apple!*

"Oh, um…*medium well*, please!" decides Trezer, trying to hurry her answer and revert to her dilemma, "Yes, something odd happened on my way over, and I had a bizarre phone call this afternoon from Mrs Cox, the headmistress at the school where I teach, who lives in the village!"

"Chicken and apple, lamb and apple, or beef and apple kebabs? Which type would you like? And do you like Moroccan cous cous? It's freshly made!"

Ezer asks everyone, much to the growing impatience of Trezer.

"All three, please!" chooses Trezer, venturing over to view Ezer's tray of food, "They look delicious, and I like your use of apple with each type of meat!"

"Chicken with golden apple, lamb with green apple, beef with red apple!"

details Ezer, placing the steaks and kebabs on the BBQ after Isaac chooses a *beef kebab*, Pip selects a *chicken kebab,* and Russet opts for a *lamb kebab!*

"Yes. Mrs Cox rang me this afternoon, ranting and raving like a mad woman!" continues Trezer, leaning into Ezer and whispering, "She's partial to a drop of apple juice…if you get my drift…and it's the school holidays! So, I couldn't take her too seriously!"

"What's that, Mum?" enquires Russet, eavesdropping - ironically when Trezer begins whispering! "What's that about Mrs Cox?"

"Oh, nothing, Russet!" answers Trezer, realising her indiscretion, "She was only saying that while she was out in her garden, pruning her bush, she spied a UFO in the sky, hovering and darting - one minute there, the next minute, gone!"

"You're joking!" remarks Pip, innocently, "A UFO?"

Isaac leans over to Pip and whispers, "And the award for *best actor* goes to…!"

"What was that Isaac?" probes Trezer, suspiciously.

"Nothing, Trezer," lies Isaac, turning the colour of his red baseball hat like a camouflaging chameleon, "I was just asking…what's a UFO!?"

"An Unidentified Flying Object!" responds Trezer, unsure whether Isaac is pulling her leg! "Mrs Cox claims she saw a UFO and says that at least five others also witnessed it...clear as day...*swear on their own lives* type of witnessing!"

"There's no such thing as UFOs!" pipes up Russet, attempting to put the conversation to bed, "That's just science fiction!"

"That's what I said to Mrs Cox," agrees Trezer, nodding, "but then when I was coming over through the cow field, an Unidentified Flying Object - yes, a UFO!" says Trezer, using her hands for dramatic effect, and looking straight at Isaac...making him fidget. "Came hurtling over, whizzing past...eerily with no noise - as silent as the blackest of black holes...heading straight this way and disappearing out of sight!"

"Two more minutes and everything is ready. Hope you are hungry!"

informs Ezer, turning the steaks and kebabs for the final time. He's been listening to the conversation but is afraid to contribute. Ezer is a useless liar...always has been and always will be!

"Don't you think that's odd?" continues Trezer, annoyed that no one else seems to be taking her seriously, "Mrs Cox, five others...me. All independently seeing a UFO on the same day!"

"Could've been one of those drones!" suggests Pip, trying to satisfy his mum's inquisition, "Taking aerial pictures of people's houses."

"Or a stunt kite," adds Russet, "caught in the wind."

"Or a piece of rubbish!" further adds Isaac, grasping at straws.

"None of those!" dismisses Trezer, perplexed by everyone's indifference, "This was big, round and gold!" describes Trezer, now turning to Ezer for support as he places everyone's food on the table, "What do you think, Ezer? Don't you find it strange?"

Ezer pauses for a moment, avoiding Trezer's gaze, and moving cutlery and crockery as if playing a game of chess. Trezer asks him again. Ezer has no choice but to blurt,

"It's the golf cart!!! We've
made a flying machine that
uses Newton's apples!"

Trezer opens her mouth but says nothing!

Isaac, Pip and Russet, on the other hand, make their feelings known, complaining to Ezer about nearly being *out of the woods* and that he's *opening a can of worms!*

Embarrassed, Ezer calls everyone to the table before the food ruins,

"Let's eat, drink and be
merry! And tell Trezer 'bout
The Flying Dolphin!"

Isaac, Pip and Russet tell Trezer everything...except the bit about the apple scrumping! They talk about Newton's apples, the chair on castors, the tractor tyre, narrowly missing Ezer, and creating The Flying Dolphin. They detail the maiden flight and Gravity Falls and convince Trezer that she, Mrs Cox and the other five villagers are not going insane as Isaac, Pip and Russet fly through every nook and cranny of this afternoon's adventure.

Trezer listens like a toddler to a bedtime story. Ezer says nothing - he's already said too much!

Occasionally, someone compliments Ezer on his food and lifts a glass of apple juice to toast his culinary skills, but overall, the meal is consumed by The Flying Dolphin!

"It all sounds so dangerous," comments Trezer as she finishes her last mouthful and moves her closed cutlery to six o'clock, worrying, "You could have all been killed!"

"We're absolute experts now!" proclaims Isaac, noting that dinner is finished, "Why don't we show you!"

"Oh, yes, Mum!" seconds Russet, smiling from ear to ear, "It's unbelievable!"

"Nothing in the whole wide world compares with The Flying Dolphin!" chips in Pip, relieved that the cat is out of the bag, "It really is one in a million!"

"Very well!" agrees Trezer, getting up from the table, "If only to corroborate your story!"

Isaac, Pip and Russet lead the way to the courtyard with Ezer and Trezer following closely behind. Isaac pulls off the red drape like a magician ripping the tablecloth from a table full of dinnerware, shouting, "Ta, dah!"

"It's wonderful," astounds Trezer, walking around and stroking The Flying Dolphin as if it's a purring cat, "It's like a space-age concept car unveiled as the car of the future to rapturous applause and high praise!"

"Why don't you take my Mum, Isaac?" suggests Russet, watching Trezer's face change from enthusiastic smiles to a look of sheer fright! "Up high into the sky and back down again,"

"And why don't you go, too, Ezer?" proposes Pip, seeing Ezer's face light up like an incandescent light bulb. "You haven't been In The Flying Dolphin yet, and it is, after all, your customised golf cart!"

"Great idea!" agrees Isaac, unlocking the clear dome, "Just up and down, Trezer - no acceleration or direction. What do you think?"

"I suppose there's no harm in it!" remarks Trezer, looking at Ezer with raised eyebrows, posing, "As long as you think it's safe, Ezer?"

"Isaac is *Captain Fantastic!* We are in his safe hands. Don't despair!"

reassures Ezer, helping Trezer into the green seat before climbing into the yellow seat.

Isaac fetches Newton's apples and removes the red apple. Handing the box to Pip, Isaac inserts the red apple into the steering post. Ezer lowers the clear dome and instructs Trezer how to close her side lock. Isaac, Trezer and Ezer apply their harnesses ready to depart.

Isaac runs through similar pre-flight checks and illuminates the edge lighting and headlight. *Evening* is morphing into *night*.

"I'd turn off the lights! We do not want any more UFO sightings!"

recommends Ezer, smiling at Trezer.

"Good thinking, Ezer!" endorses Trezer, "I don't think Mrs Cox can take another episode today!"

"Yeah, good idea," agrees Isaac, turning out the lights and gripping the red sleeve. "We can't have people finding out about The Flying Dolphin," counting down, "three, two, one, take-off!"

The Flying Dolphin shoots into the air to high pitched screams of, "GING GANG GOOLIE!" as Trezer grips her seat with white knuckles and squeezes her eyes shut.

Isaac slides the red sleeve to the neutral position and stops The Flying Dolphin. Trezer slowly opens her eyes and looks to her right to view the rear garden and beyond. Ezer looks upwards to view the stars above.

"Isn't it great!" proclaims Isaac, pointing out the village church spire. "Defying gravity at the shake of an apple!"

"This is BRILLIANT!" exclaims Trezer, acclimatising with every second.

"Look, guys! There's Venus,
and there's Jupiter - shining
bright in the night sky!"

points out Ezer, requesting Isaac to go higher.

They return home when they struggle to make out Ezer's home below. Isaac deliberately plays with Trezer's emotions as he leaves braking to the last minute! Pip and Russet can't wait to unlock the clear dome and hear their Mum's reaction.

"You were right, Pip!" acknowledges Trezer, "The Flying Dolphin certainly is *one in a million*. It's the best thing since sliced bread!"

"Let's get back to the
garden for a nightcap of
Chocolate Surprises!"

says Ezer, helping Trezer exit The Flying Dolphin. Everyone nods.

22
The Karman Line!

Trezer, Ezer, Isaac, Pip and Russet sit around the rear garden round table cupping golden droplets and delighting in the Chocolate Surprise, burping in turn to uncontrolled laughter!

"The only problem I can foresee with The Flying Dolphin," begins Trezer, patting her mouth with a napkin so as not to disturb her lipstick, "is flying without detection or raising suspicion!"

"Perhaps we should stay within Ezer's grounds," says Pip, wiping his mouth with the back of his hand.

"Or we only fly at night with the lights off," adds Russet, licking her lips then patting them dry with a napkin, "just like now, but venturing further afield."

"You will still be seen
in dark silhouette, and stand
out like a sore thumb!"

says Ezer, pragmatically, and offering more Chocolate Surprises.

"The only thing for it," begins Isaac, holding his golden droplet like a scaled down version of The Flying Dolphin, "is to turn The Flying Dolphin into a spacecraft and travel beyond prying eyes, beyond the stratosphere...into space!"

Isaac launches his golden droplet like a rocket, lifting it high into the air. The question on everyone's chocolate flavoured lips is whether it's possible.

"That sounds beyond the capability of The Flying Dolphin," says Trezer, diplomatically before cutting to the point, "and extremely dangerous!"

"Oh, Mum!" moans Pip, "Crossing the road is dangerous!"

"You may have constant
acceleration and free
energy, but you
need more than that! Like
air, and insulation, and
programmed directions!"

outlines Ezer, again pragmatically before becoming annoyed with
himself for pouring cold water on a perfectly sensible suggestion!

"I'm not saying we travel to the moon!" defends Isaac, bringing
his golden droplet back down to *earth*, "but to the edge of space
- the Karman line...where our atmosphere ends and the point
where space begins!"

"How far away is that?" enquires Russet, beginning to get cold
feet.

"My teacher, Mr Mount, says it's three hundred and thirty
thousand feet or sixty-two miles from earth," replies Isaac,
matter-of-factly.

"Sixty-two miles!" exclaims Pip, finding it difficult to fathom,
"How far is that?"

"That's like here to Cambridge," details Trezer, putting on her red
shawl as the day's heat is sucked high into the night's
atmosphere, "and that takes an hour and a half in the car...if the
traffic's good!"

"If we're accelerating at nine point eight metres per second every
second, and we take air pressure and minimal trajectory into
account - by my simple calculation, it'll take about half an hour to
reach the Karman line!"

"So, it's an hour's round trip!" calculates Russet, beginning to warm to the idea.

"I'd say an hour and a half to be safe!" responds Isaac, thinking of an analogy, "About the length of a movie!"

"Are there any downsides?" cautions Trezer, pursing her lips, "It all sounds too easy!"

"None that I can see," replies Isaac, looking to Ezer for confirmation. "What do you think, Ezer?"

"We will have to make
some modifications to
make a *space dolphin!*

If we approach it
correctly then it should be
pretty straightforward!"

replies Ezer, beginning to imagine the changes and necessary additions.

"So, its settled!" declares Isaac, holding his golden droplet and toasting, "Space. Here we come!"

"Space. Here we come!" everyone echoes, clinking their golden droplets and smiling until their cheeks begin to ache.

Isaac, Pip and Russet help Ezer by taking in the dirty plates and cutlery. As they return to the lounge area, now candle lit and calm, Pip and Russet jostle Isaac, elbowing his ribs and pushing him forwards like a sacrificial lamb!

"We were wondering, Ezer...Trezer," begins Isaac, sheepishly, "If Pip and Russet could stay the night?"

Trezer and Ezer swap glances and on Ezer's nod, Trezer replies, "Sure! Now that I've met you and discovered it's Ezer's house...how can I say *no!* You are, after all, off to space together!"

"Thanks, Mum," excite Pip and Russet, giving her a double hug and a kiss on each cheek, "You're the best!"

"Yes, yes!" replies Trezer, glancing at her watch. "And on that note, Ezer, I will bid my farewell. It's been a lovely evening - typically unconventional but genuinely lovely. Thank you!"

"Let me walk you home.
Can't have aliens abscond
you in UFO's!"

offers Ezer, helping Trezer to her feet.

"Can I take Pip and Russet on The Angry Wasp?" asks Isaac, enjoying Pip and Russet's puzzled looks, "While you take Trezer home."

"Sure! I suggest you
wear the infra-red goggles
hanging in the nest!"

replies Ezer, escorting Trezer towards the courtyard.

"Bye, Mum!" shout Pip and Russet, "See you mid-morning when you come over to the workshop to help with preparations!"

"Night, kids," bids Trezer, blowing them a kiss. "Be good!"

Isaac leads Pip and Russet in the opposite direction. The path lights up with every step, leading them through the woods until they reach The Angry Wasp's nest, lit like a smouldering flame.

Isaac claps three times. The drawbridge lowers like an alien spacecraft to reveal a pulsating inner yellow glow as if depicting inner life. Pip and Russet follow Isaac up the ramp and into the

169

inner sanctum, still none the wiser then spotting The Angry Wasp and exclaiming, "It's a roller coaster!"

"Not just a roller coaster!" defends Isaac, looking for and finding three pairs of infra-red night vision goggles, "A roller coaster that rolls and coasts through the woods! Remember the rail I pointed out that you couldn't see...well, this is it!"

"The wasp's a monster!" proclaims Pip, walking up and down to admire its detail.

"I hate wasps!" declares Russet, taking a pair of goggles from Isaac, "They spoil every picnic!"

"They actually do a lot of good!" informs Isaac, earnestly, handing Pip a pair of goggles, "They're an essential part of nature's circle of life!"

"Maybe so," adds Pip. "Tell me that when I've got three crash-landing into my apple juice!"

Pip and Isaac climb into the front seat with Russet behind and apply their infra-red goggles. As they switch them on, the nest lights automatically turn off, throwing them into pitch black. Everything adopts a monotone look with fireflies and animal eyes shining brightly. Isaac pushes the red button to lower and lock the harnesses and presses the *sound effects* yellow button!

"Everyone ready?" asks Isaac, revelling in Pip and Russet's inexperience.

"Check!" shout Pip and Russet, Pip adding, "Bring it on!"

Isaac presses the green button to start The Angry Wasp and its initial false sense of security, climbing slowly through the woods to the top of the hill. As is always the case, the nighttime experience is completely different from the daytime. Thrusting downhill in pitch black even with night vision goggles is seriously spooky as if some headless horseman will suddenly appear or sheet covered ghosts will fly by like Halloween ghoulies. The sound effects echo this, adding to the drama, and send shivers down their spines, as Isaac, Pip and Russet scream their way down the mountain and back to The Angry Wasp's nest!

"The Angry Wasp is far scarier than The Flying Dolphin!" declares Russet, holding hand on heart to feel her racing heartbeat.

"That was awesome!" yells Pip, high-fiving Isaac, "Let's do it again!"

Ezer appears, wearing black flip-flops and a long black dressing gown with gold piping and an embroidered gold flying dolphin on the left breast pocket.

"Hi, guys. Was that Good?
Who fancies a midnight swim
under moon and stars?"

"Count me in!" excites Isaac.

"And me," seconds Russet.

"I suppose The Angry Wasp can wait for another time," concedes Pip with a simple shoulder shrug, echoing, "Count me in, too!"

Ezer leads them out of the nest and through the woods along an illuminating path that turns off behind them until they reach the domed folly at the end of the rear garden. Ezer claps three times. The dome lights up and highlights a gold five-pointed star inlaid in the stone floor. Three of the five-star points point to white doors. One door has a red apple badge, another door, a green apple badge, and the third door, a yellow apple badge.

"You know your apple colours! Go change as quickly as possible, please!"

pleads Ezer, taking off his gown to reveal a red, green and yellow horizontal striped old-fashioned swimsuit.

Isaac, Pip and Russet wonder what lies in store behind each apple-emblemed door! Isaac enters the red apple changing room to find a pair of red swimming shorts, a red towel and a red thawb - a head-to-toe Arabic robe. Isaac changes into the red shorts and grabs the red towel. He exits to find Pip changed into yellow shorts and holding a yellow towel, and Russet changed into a green *all-in-one* swimsuit and holding a green towel.

Before they say anything, Ezer claps three times to illuminate the terraced water feature flowing from the foot of this fascinating folly. The top tier has an integrated deep swimming pool, fizzing with tiny bubbles, and shallower levels located at either end.

"It's beautiful!" remarks Russet, staring left and right.

"It's like being on holiday in one of those infinity pools!" adds Pip, walking to the edge and peering to the bottom to spot a large golden mosaic flying dolphin.

Without warning, Ezer dive-bombs into the pool, sending a fountain of water high into the air, splashing Isaac, Pip and Russet! Isaac follows suit, screaming, "Geronimo!" dive-bombing Ezer as he comes to the surface.

Russet takes a run up and dive-bombs Isaac as he surfaces.

Then Pip takes a run-up. He launches himself into the air to dive-bomb but then changes his mind to swallow dive. Instead, belly flopping with the largest body slap you can imagine!

They splish and splash for what seems to be an eternity until Ezer brings it to an end, saying,

"Go and dry yourselves,
and change into your coloured
thawbs for a surprise!"

"Another surprise?" says Russet, rhetorically, adding, "You are full of surprises, Ezer!"

"That's Ezer!" acknowledges Isaac, proudly, "He's *one in a million!*"

Isaac, Pip and Russet re-join Ezer, dressed in their respective robes and clutching their day clothes. Ezer has ditched his dressing gown in favour of a black thawb. He claps three times to extinguish the pool lights and illuminate a large yurt in the middle of the rear garden, announcing,

"We'll sleep under the
stars like Bedouin nomads
camping in deserts!"

"Knocks spots off a two-man tent!" remarks Pip, rubbing his hands in anticipation.

"I've always wanted to sleep in a yurt!" excites Russet, studying the intricate gold stitching in her long green sleeves.

"The closest I've got to a yurt is a plastic membraned wooden branch structure covered in layers of old and new bracken!" details Isaac, as they follow Ezer around the folly's water feature and enter the yurt through its curtain-door.

No sooner do their heads touch their makeshift pillows than they fall asleep, and Pip begins snoring like a trooper!

23
Ten to ten!

Isaac wakes with a start, perusing his surroundings in bewilderment until it dawns on him how he got to be wearing a red thawb and lying on the ground in a fabric constructed yurt. He looks over to see Pip and Russet *away with the fairies*. Ezer is nowhere to be seen.

Isaac gets up and wanders to the curtain door, flinging it open and shooting light into the yurt like a stage spotlight signifying the beginning of a play.

"Shut the door!" moans Pip, turning onto his side - huffing and puffing.

"What time is it?" enquires Russet, rising from the dead.

"Just gone eight," replies Isaac, finding Ezer's note spiked to the lawn, adding, "There's a note from Ezer."

"What's it say?" asks Russet, stirring into life - yawning and stretching her arms like a champion crossing the finishing line.

Isaac reads the note,

"I made an early
start! Please come to the workshop -
breakfast is waiting!"

"Wakey, wakey, Pip!" yells Russet, nudging him relentlessly, "Rise and shine! Ezer's already made a start on The Space Dolphin!"

Isaac, Pip and Russet change into yesterday's clothes, using their robes as mobile changing rooms! They make the short trip to the workshop to find Ezer - pleased with himself, enthusing,

"I've sealed the bottom,
and the wheels fold inwards like
airplane landing gear!"

Ezer demonstrates by flicking a dashboard lever, having raised The Space Dolphin onto jacks.

"Very clever!" praises Isaac, kneeling to watch the wheels disappear behind a flush body cover.

"So, what's next?" poses Pip, waking with every minute like a blossoming flower.

"Down-view camera,
improved steering sleeve control,
and insulation!

Then the *make or break*
issue of oxygen and
breathing equipment!"

"...AND YOUR SPACESUITS!" shouts Trezer, entering the workshop dressed in jeans and an old denim shirt showing the paint scars from previous DIY days. She has a large gold coloured holdall.

"You're early, Mum!" exclaims Russet, realising how this sounds, "I mean...we were expecting you later, but glad you're here!"

"I couldn't sit around the house, drinking tea," continues Trezer, tying her hair into a ponytail, "knowing you were all working! And, if truth be told, it's too exciting!"

Trezer, Ezer, Isaac, Pip and Russet stand around the bench, scoffing Ezer's breakfast - Chocolate Surprises with freshly baked croissants and apple turnovers. The turnovers are made with freshly picked Newton apples and shaped to suit each colour. The red apple turnovers are triangular, the yellow apple turnovers are square, and the green apple turnovers are rectangular.

"What are your thoughts on the oxygen dilemma, Ezer?" begins Isaac, starting his third turnover. Ezer has a mouthful of croissant and responds with chewed up words,

"Either single tanks...
...like scuba diving...or a...
...closed chamber...supply!?"

They discuss the merits of both, opting for the closed chamber solution and appreciating the thought of unmasked breathing.

"And what about the programming, Ezer?" enquires Russet, looking to leave no stone unturned.

"I added special
programmes to your in-helmet
navigation map!"

replies Ezer, clearly and concisely...and without croissant!

"I brought over some fabric," begins Trezer, placing her holdall on the bench and unloading offcuts from reupholstered sofas and over ordered curtain material, continuing, "I thought you should have something cool and funky!"

"We're not falling into that von Trapp!" jokes Pip, shaking his head, "And going to space dressed in drapes!"

Isaac, Pip and Russet try to suppress laughter but fail miserably! Ezer says nothing. He disappears to the far end of the workshop and returns with three rolls of contemporary red, green and yellow coloured fabric. Trezer turns from downhearted to upbeat in a second when she feels the quality of Ezer's material, admitting, "You're right, Pip! *Space Age* material for *Space Age* travel!"

They scribble ideas and designs on the whiteboard until there is a unanimous decision. Isaac, Pip and Russet want all-in-one *boiler suits* with left and right-side zips, starting at the hip and finishing on the shoulder. The front of each boiler suit is individually coloured in red, green or yellow with a black lined V-neck detail, and the back is black with a large golden flying dolphin on the shoulder blades. There are no pockets, and the sleeves come to an upturned *V* over the hand - trimmed in black. They will wear corresponding coloured baseball boots to complete the picture.

Ezer shows Trezer to his tailoring room, complete with side zips, black fabric, golden dolphin shapes and anything else she needs!

"Why don't I make a start on Russet's spacesuit while Isaac and Pip help Ezer?" suggests Trezer, giving Russet her *mother to daughter* look.

"Sounds like the perfect plan, Mum!" praises Pip, giving Trezer his *son to mother* look!

The workshop fills with focus and hard work. Ezer claps three times to play background music, alternating between *classical* and *contemporary*, occasionally injecting the virtues of *rap* and *hip-hop!*

Isaac and Pip help Ezer to carry three oxygen tanks to The Space Dolphin and position them in the side walls - on either side of the yellow and green seats, and one in the central rear. They connect them and add a single electronically controlled valve which feeds back to a dashboard gauge. Ezer comments,

"Each tank has thirty
three minutes giving air for
ninety-nine minutes!"

They insert high-tech insulation material into the side walls. Ezer adds a temperature gauge to the dashboard.

Trezer appears, grabbing everyone's attention and requesting Ezer to change the music to *2001 a space odyssey*. Ezer claps three times to blast a cloud of dry ice as Russet exits the tailoring room spacesuited and booted in green and black, and complete with a black and yellow helmet. She emerges as a space conquering heroine, cat-walking up and down the workshop like a fashion model with swagger and feline expression. Isaac and Pip holler and whistle, knowing they're next in line for a fitting!

After Trezer checks Pip's measurements to make an identical spacesuit to Russet's except in yellow, and Isaac helps Ezer to insert the downward viewing camera into The Space Dolphin, they all convene in the rear garden for lunch.

Strangely, the yurt is no longer there - just a circular witness line!

Ezer changes inconceivably quickly into Chef Strangeman and creates five Star burgers and five Chocolate Surprise Surprises - the extra *Surprise* because they are chilled milkshakes!

"Do you think we'll be ready to lift-off today?" Isaac asks Ezer and Trezer - Pip and Russet listening with bated breath.

"I'll be finished by five," responds Trezer, moving her head side to side as she estimates, concluding, "So, it's a *yes* from me!"

"Only a few more modifications. Finish by five, too. So, *yes!*"

replies Ezer, watching Isaac, Pip and Russet overflow with excitement.

"What time shall we go?" asks Russet, checking her watch.

"It has to be dark," surmises Pip, checking and reporting *sunset*, "any time after nine thirty-three!"

"I think we should lift-off at twenty-one fifty," suggests Isaac, removing his spectacles and pinching the bridge of his nose, "the date of the next seven-minute solar eclipse!"

"Ten to ten!" simplifies Trezer, liking the alliteration, "It's as good a time as any!"

"Get The Space Dolphin
set by seven. Have dinner.
Lift-off, ten to ten!"

concludes Ezer, smiling at Trezer. Everyone nods, clears the dishes and returns to the workshop.

True to her word, Trezer finishes the three spacesuits by five o'clock, and Ezer replaces the last sliding sleeve after adding additional positions for more incremental X, Y, Z direction transitions.

After wheeling The Space Dolphin into the courtyard, Ezer suggests that Isaac, Pip and Russet perform a further test flight via Gravity Falls and land where the yurt once sat in the centre of the rear garden.

Ezer carries Newton's apples empty box and helps Trezer with the three sets of spacesuits, boots and helmets. They take them to the domed folly and prepare each changing room. As they return to the lounge area, The Space Dolphin touches down in the centre of the circular witness line, and out pop Isaac, Pip and Russet, raving about the modifications and how set they are for space travel!

The sun finally waves goodnight after a prolonged dinner featuring Chef Strangeman's take on Italian Indian fusion!

Ezer changes into his beach buggy black wear. Trezer changed before dinner into a red dress with a green cardigan and gold pumps.

Isaac, Pip and Russet exit their changing rooms, dressed in Trezer's creations and holding their helmets underarm. Trezer takes a quick photo for posterity, shouting, "Say *Newton's apples!*" while Ezer stands behind her, making rabbit ears out of raised quote marks. Isaac, Pip and Russet can't help but smile!

As they walk to The Space Dolphin, the circular witness line appears to glow in the dark as if an iridescent paint has been applied to mark out a return target.

The dashboard and internal skirting lights illuminate when Isaac lifts the clear dome lid. There are no farewells only good luck wishes as Isaac, Pip and Russet take their seats, and apply their harnesses and helmets. Trezer and Ezer step back as Pip and Russet close the clear dome lid in preparation for lift-off.

Ezer hands Trezer a yellow and black *wasp* helmet, uttering,

"These allow us to
speak and see what's going on
in The Space Dolphin!"

"Cool!" replies Trezer, giggling when Ezer turns on the helmet visor and shows her which button to press to speak. Trezer tests, "Roger, Pip. Over, Russet!"

"Very good, Mum!" speaks Pip, much to Trezer's enjoyment, "Probably best if you just listen!"

"Roger, Pip. Over, Russet!" jokes Trezer, "Perhaps that's best!"

"It's twenty-one forty-nine," informs Russet after running through Isaac's checklist for the third time!

Isaac counts down, "Ten, nine, eight, seven, six, five, four, three, two, one. Lift-off!" as he raises the red sleeve and catapults The Space Dolphin into the air, away from the rapidly shrinking rear garden and into the night sky.

Gravity Falls shimmers as it reflects the starlit sky, diminishing from view as identifiable details transform into generic patches transform into a galaxy of illuminated star-like towns and villages, and planet-like cities, creating unique constellations countrywide.

Trezer and Ezer share in the wonder of Isaac, Pip and Russet from the comfort of the garden lounge area, sipping apple juice.

As the outside pressure increases and The Space Dolphin breaks through the troposphere, Isaac adjusts the oxygen outlet to maximum, instructing Pip to accelerate to three meters per second for constant vertical trajectory.

Counties turn into countries turn into continents as Isaac, Pip and Russet climb higher and higher, watching commercial aviation criss-cross and near-miss below!

The world turns into a black sea of microscopic activity. Isaac, Pip and Russet chase longitudinal sunsets as their angle of view changes and the altimeter moves ever closer to sixty-two miles.

Isaac stops The Space Dolphin when they reach the Karman line.

"We're here!" exclaims Isaac, marvelling at the curvature of the earth and its hazy atmosphere, "We're at the edge of space!"

24
One in a million!

"And that means going into orbit," adds Pip, "and that's a whole new dimension!"

"Congratulations!
You're the youngest humans to
reach the edge of space!"

reveals Ezer as if he's sitting with them in The Space Dolphin.

"Thank you, Ezer," responds Russet, "We can't tell you how beautiful it is up here!" Isaac, Pip and Russet sit and admire the view. They feel no need to fill the silent void with any noise. Instead, they revel in a shared experience that only a handful of humans have encountered.

Russet moves her sleeve left and right to alter the view. Isaac stares upwards looking for Jupiter and Venus to find the International Space Station orbiting above.

"Do you think they can see us?" asks Pip, breaking the silence.

"It's tempting to find out!" remarks Isaac, mischievously, wondering what it must be like to live in space - isolated from the world.

"Don't even think about it!" quips Russet, "We're pushing our luck travelling from the stratosphere to the mesosphere!"

"I know!" replies Isaac, "I was only joking. The International Space Station is in the thermosphere and another two hundred miles away!"

"We're getting a pretty good view through our helmets," informs Trezer, fiddling with her speech button - unaware she turns it to *open mic.*

"Hi, Mum!" shouts Pip, "We've just seen the space station!"

"We heard," replies Trezer then worrying, "I hope they don't think you're an alien spacecraft and try to blow you to smithereens!"

"You've been watching too many films!" despairs Russet, but hoping her mother is incorrect.

"How's the oxygen
level, Isaac? I think you
should start heading home!"
enquires Ezer, unable to view the dashboard gauge in his visor.

"We've used sixty-six minutes," reads Isaac, beginning to panic. "We're heading straight back. Thirty-three minutes should be enough, but it's going to be tight!"

Isaac lowers the red sleeve and instructs Pip to accelerate at the same level but in reverse. Russet orientates The Space Dolphin to point in the same direction as they came.

"Do you think they'll be OK, Ezer?" begins Trezer, thinking her conversation is private.

"It will be tight, but
they are travelling back to
oxygen and air!"
replies Ezer, directly to Trezer and inaudible to the others.

"There's something I need to tell you, Ezer," continues Trezer, still unaware that her words are broadcast to The Space Dolphin.

Isaac, Pip and Russet aren't paying much attention, focusing on the task in hand - getting home safely!

Ezer studies Trezer, wondering what she has to say.

"What colour is your hair?" asks Trezer, bizarrely as if to change the subject, but continuing before Ezer has a chance to reply, "And what colour is the hair of Pip and Russet?"

Ezer says nothing but his face says it all as it turns from a look of concern for the safety of The Space Dolphin to a look of shock as his mouth opens, his eyes widens, and he grips his chin.

You can hear a pin drop in The Space Dolphin. Isaac watches the altimeter drop further and further. The oxygen gauge exhales precious minutes as Pip and Russet inhale deeply, hanging on a cliffs' edge and waiting for the punchline.

It doesn't take a rocket scientist to work it out.

"Pip and Russet are your children!" blurts Trezer, relieved that the truth is out. The truth she's been carrying for years, and the guilt that Ezer never knew.

Isaac expects Pip and Russet to say something, but they remain silent - shell-shocked by this bombshell.

Ezer eventually says something.

"Why did you not come
back as soon as you knew? Let
me be their father?"
enquires Ezer, out of earshot.

"I can't explain why," admits Trezer, awkwardly, "and then we moved away, and it felt like it was for the better!"

Pip begins to hyperventilate.

"You better take a few hits from your inhaler," suggests Russet, watching Pip struggle to draw breath.

Pip reaches down to his pockets, remembering there are no pockets, and that his inhaler is in his jeans - hanging up in the yellow apple changing room!

Pip gives Russet a look that she's seen before - the look of fear and alarm. He must get a hit from his inhaler, or the consequences could be dire.

"We've got to get back, Isaac!" screams Russet, "Pip needs his inhaler!"

"Ezer, we have a problem!" says Isaac through his helmet, trying to remain calm, "Pip is panicking, and needs his inhaler which is in his jeans...hanging up in the changing room."

"Are you OK, Pip?" enquires Trezer, anxiously, "Try to remain calm and don't chase your breath."

"We know your secret, Mum!" exclaims Russet, unable to contain herself.

"Know what secret, Russet?" probes Trezer, suddenly realising her error with the helmet speech button.

"That Ezer is our Dad!" proclaims Russet with a mixture of annoyance and happiness, repeating, "Ezer, you are our Dad!"

"I'm so sorry, Pip and Russet," apologises Trezer, taking a huge bite of humble pie, "I didn't want you to hear like this!"

"The inhaler will
be here when you return. Keep
calm everybody!"

advises Ezer, knocked for six by Trezer's announcement, adding,

"Pip. Russet. I can't
tell you how happy I am
to be your father!"

Ezer fetches Pip's inhaler and returns to Trezer. They hug.

Russet holds Pip's hand and tries to coach him through this frightening episode. The time seems to tick by at a snail's pace even though the altimeter races down like a hare escaping the hunters' gun.

Incapacitated, Pip can't control his yellow sleeve correctly, and The Space Dolphin veers off course. There are three minutes to go with three minutes of oxygen.

"Ezer, we have another problem," radios Isaac, "We're off course and by my calculations, heading straight for Gravity Falls!"

"Don't panic. Maintain
your course. We'll meet you there.
The Dolphin will float!"

responds Ezer, grabbing Trezer's hand and leading her to the beach buggy. Ezer slams it into reverse then kicks it into first gear and tears up the hill, changing up and down the gears as they navigate through the woods and up to Gravity Falls. They reach the boathouse with thirty-three seconds to spare.

"Brace yourselves, Pip, Russet!" yells Isaac, as he pulls the red sleeve to its neutral position...a few seconds too late as they dive bomb into the lake and head for Gravity Falls!

The impact throws Isaac forwards. He hits his head on the dashboard and knocks himself out!

Meanwhile, Trezer and Ezer run around the lake to see The Space Dolphin shoot off Gravity Falls. They manage to get down to the lower pool just as The Space Dolphin surfaces and floats over to the side.

"Pip, Russet. Isaac!" yells Trezer, helping Ezer to unlock the side latches and lift the clear dome lid, "Are you OK?"

"We're fine," replies Pip, taking a large dose from his inhaler, "but Isaac's not!"

"He hit his head when we landed on the lake at the top of Gravity Falls!" concerns Russet, unclipping her harness, "He hasn't said a word since..."

"Isaac...you OK?
It's Ezer, Uncle Ezer.
Wake up! Please, wake up!"

shouts Ezer, shaking Isaac's shoulders and feeling his neck for a pulse...

"Isaac...you OK?
It's Ezer, Uncle Ezer.
Wake up! Please, wake up!
How long have you been
like this? Why did I leave you
to fetch a motor!?"

shouts Ezer, placing Isaac in the recovery position by Newton's tree and listening to his chest for signs of breathing as he spies three apples lying innocently on the ground...

"Isaac...you OK? You are...Isaac? Isaac Newman?" enquires a man standing over Isaac - sat on his green trunk outside the school changing rooms and looking down as if deep in thought, "It's your uncle. Your father's cousin. John Newman!"

Isaac stirs from his daydream, removing his spectacles to rub his eyes with the back of his hand. He replaces his spectacles and looks up, focusing on a tall man with short orange-red hair and the friendliest of smiles. Isaac finally computes and responds, "Yes. I'm Isaac. Excuse me - I was away with the fairies! Having the most amazing and vivid daydream!" continues Isaac, standing up and shaking his uncle's hand, "Pleased to meet you, Sir!"

"Less of the *Sir!* Call me, John!" replies Isaac's uncle, lifting Isaac's trunk. "Apologies for being so late, but the traffic was against us all the way, and the *satnav* stopped working fifteen minutes after we departed!"

"No problem!" smiles Isaac, "I'm delighted to have someone...correction, *family!* To stay with for the summer holiday, and what's another hour or so after a whole term!"

"Let's put your trunk in the boot and then I'll introduce you to my family," continues John, clicking his remote control to open the car boot automatically.

Isaac studies the car. It's a gold metallic SUV, possibly Japanese or Swedish, with all-terrain wheels and tinted windows. There's a small sticker on the rear window. It reads *Save The Dolphin* with a graphic image of a blue dolphin, *flying* out of the sea.

John opens the rear side door, uttering, "Move up kids. Make room for Isaac. There's plenty of room for three in the back!"

Isaac grins at the other two children - a girl and a boy, both with orange-red hair and similarly aged to him. John climbs into the driving seat and shuts his door, announcing in a deep voice, "Everyone, meet Isaac...and Isaac, meet my wife, Joan, and the twins, Philip and Rosanne!"

"It's lovely to meet you finally," greets Joan, giving Isaac a heartfelt smile to reveal perfect white teeth framed by bright red lipstick, "It's funny how families can be so near and yet so far! It's a shame that your parents couldn't make it, but I know two very excited people who are delighted to have someone to spend the summer!" she continues, straining to look at Philip and Rosanne. Joan has black hair, blue eyes and exudes a natural calmness. Isaac thinks she has the look of a mother if there's such a thing!

"Call me, Pip!" says Philip, giving Isaac a welcoming smile, "Everyone else does!"

"And call me, Russet!" says Rosanne, leaning forwards to stare at Isaac, and tugging her orange-red forelocks, "On account of my orange-red hair!"

"Right. Is every one seat belted?" continues John, glancing at everyone's laps, "Very good. Let's make a movie!"

John makes a three-point turn in the vacant car park and heads up the school drive, turning on the in-car stereo to belt out *Beethoven's fifth symphony*, immediately turning it down to second guess Joan.

"You must be hungry, Isaac," presumes Joan, lifting a canvas bag from between her legs, "I've got a selection of apples to keep our hunger at bay until we get home."

"I'll have a green apple, please, Mum," orders Russet, collecting her green apple from Joan's hand.

"I'll have a golden apple, please, Mum," orders Pip, collecting his golden apple from Joan's hand.

Pip and Russet aren't identical twins, but they have similar mannerisms and turn of phrase.

"I've never had a choice before," admits Isaac, looking at Joan holding out a red apple, "but red's a great colour. I'll have a red apple, please!"

"John can't eat apples," informs Joan, taking a bite out of her green apple and turning to John. "Can you, dear?"

John nods and makes a left turn out of the school gate.

"It makes his lips swell up like balloons, and brings him out in a rash," adds Russet, pulling a face of disgust and making her upper body shiver as if someone has walked over her grave.

"It can be more serious than that," contributes Pip, "You can get anaphylaxis, Dad. Can't you?"

"That's right!" confirms John, sighing deeply. "I wish I could eat apples, but unlike *Sleeping Beauty* who wakes from a single kiss, one bite could put me to sleep forever!"

"It's what makes you special, dear," confirms Joan, giving him a warm smile. "Your apple allergy makes you *one in a million!*"

THANK YOU FOR READING

I HOPE YOU ENJOYED AS MUCH AS I ENJOYED WRITING

ISAAC AND NEWTON'S APPLES

GAVIN THOMSON

MMXVIII

I

31755637R00110

Printed in Poland
by Amazon Fulfillment
Poland Sp. z o.o., Wrocław